FALLING FOR A BLACK *Billionaire*

A SHORT STORY BY

BIANCA

PREVIOUSLY

Kriss Brown

First, they smile in your face, then they tell you how good your resume looks, then they tell you that they can't hire you, and then tell you that they wish you the best. How the hell can you wish me the best when you wouldn't give me the job? How can you tell me how good my resume looks, but then won't hire me? Don't tell me how good my resume is, then tell me that you can't hire me. I know my credit is bad... I know that I have student loans out the ass. I know that. Don't remind me. That don't mean I'm going to steal from your bank. I have much more class than that. My dad raised me better than that. I don't steal and I hate people who do.

After leaving out of the tenth bank in two weeks that turned me down, I sighed. I would call my dad, Charlie Brown, but I would see him in a few minutes, so I could tell him face to face. Gon' head and laugh at my dad's name. People been laughing at his name since grade school, and since Chris Brown became a thing, they laugh at my name too. Yes, my name is Kriss Brown. Nope, it's not short for anything. It's just Kriss. Even when I put that on my resume, people still call out 'Kristina.'

No lady. If that was my name, I would have put it down on the paper. Excuse me for being hostile, I'm just upset that I thought that I would be able to quit my damn job tonight. I'm a bottle girl and waitress at Club 227. Don't get me wrong, the money is great, but I would much rather be in my field.

I graduated from Spelman at the top of my class two years ago. I graduated with a bachelor's and master's in accounting. I minored in finance. So, I was good in numbers. I was president of many math clubs on campus. I was a math tutor for my work study job. My stellar background didn't supersede these student loans and bad credit though. I'm like, how can I work on my student loans and bad credit if I don't get a job? I would have had a college fund if my mom hadn't died giving birth to me. *She* was Kristina Brown. The only thing I had of her was pictures.

I look just like her. Five-nine, petite, and chocolate. My long legs were holding up a tight and toned ass, and my chest was holding up a pair of 38 DDs. I even got my hair from her because she wasn't fully black. She was black and Latina, so my hair was thick and down my back. I kept it in big thick curls, so my hair could stop at my shoulders. Being able to pass for eighteen is a blessing and a curse. I get carded everywhere I go, even though I am twenty-seven years old.

Anyways, my college fund was depleted because the cleaner business that my mom and dad owned together had to be closed because my dad didn't want to run it by himself. He said that it wouldn't be the same. He always bragged about my mom's love for numbers... and that's where I got it from. I don't fault him at all because being a single dad was hard for him. He never remarried even though I told him I would be okay with him being with someone else. He said that it wouldn't be the same.

"Excuse me. No loitering," the security guard said. "It looks suspicious that you have been standing out here for the last fifteen minutes."

I gave him the ugliest look before moving two steps down away from in front of the bank and sat on a bench to take a load off.

"Happy now? Fat ass!" I hissed his way.

My phone beeping stopped me from going off on the fat ass man some more. I pulled it out of my purse and it was a message from one of my best friends Lawrynn to our 'Besties' group chat.

Law: Hey, Krissy Pooh. How did the interview go? I know you killed it.

Russ: Yes, I was getting ready to text that as well. How was it?

Russ, short for Russell, was my other best friend. Him, Lawrynn, and I met at this social that someone was throwing for both Morehouse and Spelman our freshman year of college. We been tight ever since. Lawrynn also attended Spelman but we hardly ever seen each other because she wanted to be a lawyer, so her buildings were on the other side of the campus. Russ went to Morehouse, and he was getting a degree in engineering, so we only had a chance to really kick it on weekends. Now that we are all graduated, and both Lawrynn and Russ are getting settled into their careers, we kick it a lot more.

Me: Can y'all talk?

Moments later, my phone was ringing and it was Law. I answered and she put me on hold to call Russ.

"Hey my beauties! What's going on, Kriss? Please don't tell me they gave you that bullshit excuse again," he sighed into the phone.

"Yes! They did. Y'all... I'm so tired of this shit. I had a whole speech ready for my stupid ass boss tonight at work."

"What was ya speech, Kriss?" Lawrynn asked chuckling.

"Hell, I was gon' tell him to kiss my ass and shoot him two middle fingers."

"You are acting like Nardo's ass wouldn't love to do that anyway. You the best-looking girl he has there. He will do anything to keep you there," Russ laughed.

"Forget Nardo! I can't stand him. He's the worst kind of rich guy," I sighed.

"Honestly, you might need to ride his stick... and get some of that money," Law laughed.

Leonardo Aubin was a billionaire... and of course he opened a club where mostly billionaire's hang. Most of the females that work there have had sex with him, and they hate me because I didn't have to do that to get the job. Don't get me wrong, Nardo is fine as hell. He's tall, dark chocolate, with a body that only God could have sculpted out himself. He has these thick lips that he is always licking like he thinks it's a mating call for women. His teeth are so straight and white and when he notices you looking at them, he runs his thick, pink ass tongue across them. His eyes are light brown and he has eyelashes and eyebrows that women envy. He keeps his hair in a fade.

Nardo also has a huge magic stick. I know because I have seen it. It literally sits on his thigh and you can tell in every pair of pants that he wears... doesn't matter what kind of pants he wore. I saw it in person when he 'accidently' sent it to me. He swore he meant to send it to another woman, but I got it. I only put up with Nardo's antics because I made gooood money at 227. Did I mention that he was Haitian? I would never date a Haitian man again. They are the devil's spawn. Trust me. My ex, Malcolm, is a Haitian.

"I'll have sex with Russ before I have sex with Nardo."

"Wait! Can we set that up?" Russ laughed.

"Shut-up, Russ!"

Russ was a dog and would have sex with anything that moved. I would never put our friendship in that type of state.

"Look, I'm going to go visit my dad at Ground-Up. Are you guys going to come by 227 tonight? I'm not working that long tonight. I'll get off around two and we can sit and have drinks. I need one, two, or five," I said to them.

"Hell yeah! I'm down. I need to find me a billionaire sugar mama. I'll just have to hold my breath while I knock the dust off that gray-haired vagina."

"Russ, you'll stick your thang in anything and quite frankly, it's sad. I can't wait until you wake up with your dick next to you and it's shriveling up and dying, and the doctors can't save it," Lawrynn said, making me burst into a fit of laughter, making other people stop on the sidewalk and look at me.

"Damn, Law. I'll kill myself if that happened. I'll see y'all later. I just got an order," Russ said and hung up.

"I'll see you later, Krissy!" Lawrynn said and blew me a kiss into the phone before she hung up.

I put my phone in my purse and took out my ballerina flats. I was not about to walk five blocks in six inch heels. I needed to save some of my strength so I could walk in the heels tonight. I exchanged shoes and stood up. I put in my earbuds and turned on my favorite song "I Feel It Coming" by The Weekend.

I had walked five blocks without nothing or nobody bothering me. I made it to the last crosswalk and as soon as the sign told me it was my time to walk, this big ugly ass Rolls Royce stopped in the middle of the crosswalk. I walked up to the hood of the car, hoping they would back up, but nope. Whoever was in it, didn't back up. So, I took a few steps back and then lifted my leg and proceeded to walk across the hood of the car. I could see the people in the crosswalk laughing. My music was not loud, so I heard the voice.

"AYE, YOU STUPID WHORE! WHAT THE HELL IS YOUR PROBLEM?" the voice yelled.

Turning around, snatching my earbuds out my ear, I yelled at the driver, "NEXT TIME, DON'T PULL YOUR CAR INTO THE CROSSWALK. DO IT AGAIN, AND I'LL WALK OVER YOUR BIG UGLY CAR AGAIN!"

I put my earbuds back in my ear, shot him two middle fingers, and turned around to continue my journey. Ten minutes later, I was walking into Ground-Up Enterprise, where my dad was a full-time janitor. All he knows is cleaning, so after he closed his cleaning business, he just got two full-time cleaning jobs. He was also a full-time janitor at my old elementary school. The two jobs never run over because he works during the day at the elementary school, evenings, afternoons, and some nights at Ground-Up. He gets frequent breaks from the school because they get out of school now, for anything.

I know people look down on jobs like a janitor but my dad makes good money at both jobs. Ground-UP values their employees, so he can take a break whenever he wants or days off with no penalties and as long as the excuse is valid.

I grabbed my visitor badge and walked through the metal detector. This building is ten stories high and all I know is that some people in here do architect shit. I never knew that you needed a building this big to draw shit. I don't even understand why people need security in an architect building, but that is none of my business. I stopped at the man who looks at the cameras.

"Hey, can you tell me what floor Charlie Brown, the janitor, is on?" I asked the man.

He looked at me as if he wanted to laugh, until he saw my face, then he brought those curly lips down to a flat line. He looked at the cameras for a minute.

"He's on the third floor and he just went into office twelve," the man said.

"Thanks."

I rounded the corner to the elevator and this man was getting on there.

"Hold the elevator," I said.

This man looked at me and climbed onto the elevator, and I was thinking that he was going to hold the doors for me, but he didn't. As soon as I got to the doors of the elevator, he was pushing the button so the doors could close even faster. I got a good look at his face before the door closed because if I ever saw him again, I was going to curse him out so bad, his ears were going to bleed. I looked up and saw that he was going to the tenth floor.

I couldn't do anything but sigh. This day was so bad.

Travis Spencer III (Spence)

*D*id I feel sorry for closing the door on that loud ghetto chick with the big hair? Hell no, because that was the girl that hiked across the top of my goddamn car. I had just gotten my car waxed and she did that shit. I wouldn't ever forget those damn curls and those long ass middle fingers she threw up at my driver. I was looking at her through my heavily tinted back window. I prayed to God that she wasn't one of the new architects that I was hiring today. I had to give the architect I fired a healthy severance package because she couldn't handle the sex I put down on her and she got crazy. My dad told me that I was never supposed to get my pussy where I get my paycheck because that's how shit gets out of hand. I had messed around with a lot of these women that work here and she was the only one that got out of hand.

I made it to the tenth floor and got off the elevator. This whole floor belonged to me and my team of architects and our assistants. You had to have a code to get to the tenth floor.

"Good morning, Spence," my assistant spoke to me.

"Good morning, Zahara. How many interviews do I have today?"

"You only have two interviews today. One is in thirty minutes and the other one is in an hour. I have their resumes here for you, if you would like to go over them," she responded.

"Bring them to my office in about ten minutes. I need to have my coffee before I look at anything work related."

"Got it."

Opening my office door, I stepped inside the huge space, then sat my briefcase down before removing my suit jacket and hanging it up. Zahara had already set my coffee on my desk. I took one sip and my body came alive. Ground-Up Enterprise was started by my grandfather Travis Spencer. He gave it to my father Travis Spencer II when he was thirty and my father passed it down to me when I was thirty. I hated when people called me Mr. Spencer because that makes me feel old, so, I have them call me Spence.

I remembered when I was seven years old, my dad put a pencil in my hand and gave me a graph. He started making me learn how to draw, even when I expressed interested in cooking. When normal kids were outside playing and watching cartoons on Saturday mornings, I was drawing. I hated it but I learned to love it over time. Every night, I would sneak and watch cooking shows. I don't know why I loved cooking, but I did. I had two younger siblings, Trevor Spencer who is thirty, and Trena Spencer who is twenty-seven.

Trevor has an office down the hall from me and Trena spends all her time spending the family's money. My dad didn't put a pencil in her hand like he did myself and Trevor. He lets her do whatever she wants to do. She's been in and out different universities. Never held down a job. Never done anything worth mentioning, and my dad doesn't care. He coddles her. After her third car accident, I stopped giving her money for anything. Trevor is at his wits' end with her as well.

Knock! Knock!

"It's open!" I called out.

"Here are the resumes for today. I hope you find what are you are looking for, Spence, and if not, we have two hundred resumes we have to go through," Zahara spoke after stepping into my office.

"Maybe one of these will work out," I responded to her.

She left me to myself.

I opened the file and the first interview was a woman around the age of twenty-five. I shook my head because I'm sure this interview was the big hair ghetto woman that I closed the elevator on. Actually, I was hoping it was her because I wanted to tell her to her face that I would never hire a rude ass woman like her. It was a good thing that I wasn't going to hire her because the last twenty-five-year-old I hired, was the woman that I had to fire because she couldn't handle us having sex and continuing to work together.

She became too clingy. Dangerously clingy at that. Bust your windows out and key your car type clingy. Trevor always told me that these young women were going to be the death of me and that I should find me a nice, age appropriate woman to settle down with. I'm forty years old, no kids, never been married, or any of that. I know I'm a good catch... but I would much rather play the field. Playing the field is much more fun than being married. I don't think I want kids anyway. Too stressful and plus, I work odd hours of the day. I wouldn't have any time for them. Just a lot.

I kicked back and waited for Miss Monique, the ghetto big hair girl to come in, so I can read her for filth and then rip her resume up in her face. The knocks came just when I expected them to and I told them to come in. I almost choked when Zahara didn't escort the big haired ghetto girl in. I had to sit up and straighten my tie. I stood and shook her hand and told her to have a seat. Monique was beautiful, but not who I expected.

"Hello, Spence. My name is Monique and I am here to interview for the entry-level architect job. I have my portfolio here, if you would like to take a look," she said.

She listens very well. I'm sure Zahara told her that I don't like to be called Mr. Spencer. I reached for her portfolio and flipped threw it slowly. Her work looked very good. She looked like she would be a great asset to Ground-Up. I would have to look at the other guy that was going to interview after her.

"I really love your work, Miss Monique. We'll be in touch, if we are interested."

"That's it?" she asked, looking confused. "No questions. Just going to peek at my portfolio."

"Precisely. The only thing I need to know is if you can draw. You can do that. Now, I'll be in touch if we are interested," I said, and stood to indicate that the interview was over.

"Okay, Spence."

She took her portfolio from me and left out of my office. See, to work here, you must have an upbeat attitude. I don't ask questions because I want people to sell themselves to me. She didn't do that. You have to be able to make our customers feel confident in our work. You don't wait for your customers to ask questions. You sell yourselves to them so good to the point where they won't even have questions until you are laying out the blueprint to draw their house or whatever.

The second interview is a guy by the name of Mr. Chadwick Grant. I had a few minutes before my next interview. For some odd reason, I wanted to know why the big hair girl was here. I called down to my brother's office to see if he was hiring someone. He answered on the first ring.

"Big bro, what's going on?" he answered the phone.

"Are you hiring someone today?"

"No. My team down this way is good. Why you ask?"

"Do you know if Selena is hiring anyone today?" I asked him.

Selena hires for the other positions in the company. My brother and I hire all the architects but we leave everything else from security, to accounting, to janitors, and whatever else to Selena. Selena is a good friend of mine from college. She is also one of the few women here that I have not smashed.

"Nah, I don't know. You want me to call down there and ask her?"

"I got it," I said and hung up.

I picked up the phone and again called down to Selena's office and she picked up on the first ring.

"Yes, Spence."

"Are you hiring someone today?"

"No, I'm not. You were the only person that had interviews today. Why you ask?"

"No reason," I said and hung up the phone.

I don't know why it bothered me so bad to know who she was when she wasn't shit to me. My phone rang and it was Zahara.

"Yes."

"Hey, I was just calling to let you know that Chadwick had to cancel his interview because his grandfather just died moments ago. I told him to call when everything is over to see if the position was still open and if so, I'll schedule him."

"Great," I said and hung up.

I grabbed my coat off the back of the chair and left out of my office. I quickly passed by Zahara's desk before she could ask me where I was going. When I got on the elevator, I pressed the first floor and leaned against the wall to wait.

Ding.

The elevator stopped on the third floor and when the doors opened, I looked into the face of her.

The *her* with the big hair. The very tall, dark skinned *her*. The *her* who I now know has very long legs attached to a nice size waist, who had my mouth watering at the thought of what's behind her. The *her* who had a pair of watermelons on her chest that I would love to lay my head on. At this current moment, the *her* who is giving me the ugliest look I had ever received from a woman before.

Kriss

The chat that I had with my father went well. He gave me a huge hug and a big kiss on my forehead and told me that he was proud of me anyhow. He told me that I was the best daughter that anyone could ever ask for. He was also saddened because he felt like it was his fault because he depleted my college fund while trying to get his life together after becoming a widow and a new dad at the same time. I would never fault him for doing what he had to do as a father. I still got two degrees.

We didn't talk long because his breaks were short. I would have come later, but I needed to take me a nap before I had to go to work. You don't know how much energy you need to serve billionaires. They are so arrogant, rude, needy, and think that just because they got money, you are supposed to bow down to them. I would never do that shit. Why you think I hadn't had sex with Nardo's ass. Don't get me wrong, those billionaires will throw that money for sex, but I'm just not that desperate yet. I'll just take their tips for now, and when I have these girls on my chest out, they tip very well.

After my dad kissed me on my forehead again, I told him that I would see him if he comes home before I leave for work. I stood in front of the elevator and waited for the doors to open. When the doors opened, I saw *him*. The *him* that closed the elevator doors on me when I first made it here. I looked him up and down in his fancy tailored suit. You could tell that he worked out because his body was so muscular.

He looked to be the same height as my dad, who is 6'5. He had a thick mustache and a beard that was lined to perfection. His hair was cut low with waves you could swim in. The color of his skin was the same as mine, with no blemishes. Looking him up and down, you could tell that he took very good care of himself on the outside, but the inside was very rotten. My face turned into a scowl when I noticed that he was salivating at my breast.

"I'll take the next one," I calmly said and started looking at my phone.

"Why?" he replied in a very deep baritone voice.

A voice so deep that I'm sure in the bedroom, he makes a lot of panties moist.

"Because I just had the best chat with the best man in the world and it has me feeling on cloud nine, and I don't want to damper my mood being in the presence of a bastard like yourself. Because, I know that if I get on the elevator, I will curse your ass out for closing the doors on me earlier when I *first* encountered you. Because I know myself, and I know that if I get on that elevator, I will end up having to tell you that I will carve your heart out of your chest and grind it up in my blender to have it with my morning shake," I said to him, and his mouth fell into an O shape, showcasing a very thick, pink tongue.

Smiling, I said, "So, again, I'll take the next one."

Ding.

He let the doors close while he still had that shocked look on his face.

"Girl, do you know who that was?" the lady next to me said, who

I didn't even notice had come and stood next to me.

"No, and I don't care to know who he was," I huffed and walked away, deciding to take the stairs.

I put my earphones on and walked away from the lady. I made it to the lobby, and I saw the guy from the elevator looking at me. His lips were moving, but I reached into my pocket and turned my music up louder, hoping that hearing my music would be his cue to keep his lips together. I returned my visitor's badge and walked out of the door. I wanted to look behind me, to get a glimpse of his butt in those slacks, but I wouldn't give him the satisfaction of looking behind me.

I took an Uber home because I do not drive if I have to park downtown. It costs a fortune, and the Uber ride to and from the home I share with my father is much cheaper. We stayed in the house that I grew up in. It was a two-story, four bed, and three bath brick home. The house was paid for, and I didn't see myself needing to move out. My dad doesn't invade my space, and I don't invade his. The whole upstairs is mine, and he barely comes up here.

I got out of my interview clothes, washed my face free of make-up, and got in the bed. Today was Friday, and I'm sure the men were going to be bothering me like crazy. I gave all my burdens to God before I drifted off into a peaceful sleep.

5 hours later

I was standing in the mirror in the locker room perfecting my Fenty Beauty Stunna Lip Paint. I was so happy Rihanna came out with this because these deep red lips and chocolate color skin drove these men up in here wild. My outfit tonight was a red, lace, crystalized lingerie set that I had custom made. I had a white crop tank top tee to go over it and a short white skirt to go over my lace cheeky panties. I had to put on my last coat of body glitter before I put it on.

Every girl that worked here wore next to nothing as a work uniform. I had no problem with it because I'm not ashamed of my body at all. Club 227 was basically a gentleman's club if you will. I know for a fact that these raggedy ass men were paying Nardo to have sex with some of these girls because one of them tried to pay him to get me that way. I smacked the hell out of Nardo and told him I'd kill him if he ever tried to auction me off again.

"Damn, you are looking hot, mama. I wish you would get your ass up on that pole with me. Do you know how much money you could get? You know that those men love them a good piece of thick chocolate," JuJu said to me and pinched my ass.

Juju was an Asian who was trying to pay her way through school. JuJu's real name was Akira. I don't know how she got that out of Akira, but if it floats her boat, it's all good. She was also one of the only ladies here who accepted me. The other ladies hate me because I don't have to strip to get all the tips, and I definitely didn't have to have sex with Nardo to continue working here. She was pleased that I was one of the only ladies who could keep Nardo in check. She said she couldn't resist his charm and she broke down and had sex with him and was happy that I wasn't weak like the rest of the girls there, including her.

"Girl. I don't want to dance for no white men who fetishize me. I barely want to walk around in this in front of them, but this is what's paying the bills, for now, before I start working on my student loans."

"Oh yeah, how did that interview go?" she asked me.

Before I could breathe a word to her, Nardo came around the corner.

"What interview, Krimson?" Nardo asked, calling me by my stage name.

I chose Krimson because I always wore some variation of red every night because my favorite color is red.

I ignored him and was about to start talking back to JuJu, but she scattered from the locker room. Ugh, I hate that these women fear him. He walked up behind me as I was sticking my eyelashes on.

"Kriss," he hissed. "Are you actively looking for employment?"

I rolled my eyes to the ceiling because he knew I was. I let him know that every chance I got.

"Yes, I am. You knew I wasn't going to spend the rest of my life working here. I do have two degrees."

"But you have only been here for two years. I don't mistreat you or anything, do I?" he asked, reaching in front of me to grab my glitter oil.

Men.

"You sexually harass me every day, Nardo. You make very nasty remarks towards me and the other girls here," I paused when I felt him rubbing the oil on my ass. "See, like now. I didn't ask you to rub my oil on me. We have a lady who does that. Where is Leola?"

Leola was the den mother of the girls. She kept us oiled up and did everything from our hair down to our make-up if we needed it. I never let anyone touch my face. I have let her do my hair a few times, but that's it.

"Leola is in my office," he said as he started rubbing my back.

"I bet she is," I whispered.

"Listen," he said and turned me around. "You are a beautiful girl, and I wish that I could date you. If you have to leave for us to date, then I'll let you go."

"Ewe, I wouldn't date you even if I didn't work here. And, what you mean, *let me go?* I can leave whenever I want."

"On the contrary... you signed a contract giving me four years of your life. So, unless you want to buy out of that contract," he paused, closed what little space we had between us and leaned over to speak into my ear, "which I know you won't, because you don't have the cash to do so, I suggest you get with the program."

His ear was close to my mouth, so I decided to speak into his ear like he was doing me. He was trying to intimidate me.

"Leonardo Aubin, I know exactly what I signed. I know how to read. If I want to give you two years, then I'll give you two years. I also know that you be pimping these girls to the highest bidder, and I just know that APD, also known as Atlanta Police Department, would love to know what you are doing in here. I can see the headlines now, 'Billionaire *black* man, Nardo Aubin, arrested for running a prostitution ring out of his club.' So, if you don't back away from me..." I growled, and he took a few steps back from me, not even giving me a chance to finish my statement.

During our intense stare down, I snatched my oil from him and turned back around. I could see him in the mirror staring at me while I put my top on. I had to bend over to step in my skirt, and he stood there and stared at me.

"One day, I'll wear you down Kriss, and I'mma have your ass wrapped around my finger."

"That'll be on the thirty-first of February. If you ain't worn me down in two years, why you think... never mind. Have a good night," I said, walking away from him and walking out to the bar.

"Damn, you so sexy," Miguel, the guy who ran the bar, said to me when I approached him. "I know I don't make a billion dollars but... I make a smooth sixty thousand. Is that enough to date you?" he asked and started laughing before pulling me into a hug.

Miguel and I would always harmlessly flirt with each other, but we both knew that we would never get with each other.

"Listen, you know we got a packed house tonight. So, make sure you are on your P's and Q's. How are you feeling? You need a shot or two?"

"Nah, I am waiting until I get off. I am not working that long tonight."

"Girl, I see why these girls envy you. You do what you want because you know Nardo ain't going to do shit."

Nardo don't scare me and I been letting him know that since day one," I said, grabbing the first bottles off the tray.

After four hours, I was two thousand dollars richer after counting my tips while I put them in a rubber band and stuffed them in my bag. I put on my jumpsuit that I wore into work and walked out the locker room to find my friends. They were there at two o'clock, just like they said they would be, and I was happy to see that they had already ordered me three shots because I needed it.

Spence

The rest of the day at work, I couldn't help but to think about Miss Ghetto with the big hair telling me that she would carve my heart out and grind it up with her morning protein shake. I never had a woman talk to me like that before. I bet if she knew who I was, she would have changed her tune. I had to play it off when I saw her coming out of the staircase because I didn't want her to know that I was specifically looking for her. I was making meaningless conversation with the front door people when she walked up to return her visitor's badge. I was trying to talk to her, but she purposely turned her music up on her headphones. I was low-key embarrassed when she ignored me in front of the front desk personnel.

"Who was that girl? She's rude and apparently doesn't know who you are. Was that your interviewee?" Selena asked me, but I was too fixated on her slim backside to answer her.

"Spence!" Selena said, snapping her fingers in my face.

"Yes... Yes, Selena? I have no idea who she is. I don't care to know who that rude lady is," I snapped and walked off.

I wanted to check the check-in book to get her name, but I ain't want to appear thirsty. I went back up to my office to see if I could get some work done.

I know you may think that the security cameras and check-in books are a bit obsessive, but I have to be that way. There are other companies that have been trying to sabotage my grandfather's company since the beginning of time. They hated to see my grandfather, a black man born to two black parents, succeed in a mostly white field. He taught himself how to draw, and it started from there. One time, this company called Designs for You tried to send somebody in here to steal our designs. I wanted to break every one of those Mason brothers' white noses, but I hit them where it hurts... their pockets.

I sued them for five million and got all my money and donated it to my HBCU Morehouse. Don't even get me started on the Archibald brothers. They tried to send their sister to do their dirty work, as if I messed around with white women, let alone dated them. I wanted to sue them, but my lawyer said I couldn't prove that, so I left them alone, but I got a feeling they will be back with some stupid shit one day, and I will be ready.

After I had been working for a few hours, I heard a knock on my door and told the person to come in.

"Yo, you trying to go with the crew to 227 tonight? It's Friday, so you know it's going to be live in there. I need to relieve some stress," my brother said to me.

"Yeah, I do... but let me get this project three fourths done because I had a deadline of getting this done tomorrow, and I know those shots of Patron are going to have me lit. Give me about forty-five minutes," I said to him.

He nodded his head and closed my door. Trevor was the spitting image of me and our father. The only difference between us was that he was a little smaller than me because he doesn't lift as much weight as I do, and he wore his hair in that childish hair cut with the braids in the middle of his head, and the rest of his hair shaved down the sides. He was too damn old to be wearing his hair like that. I called my driver, Rick, to let him know the plans, and then I picked up the phone to call Nardo.

"Yeah, boss!" he picked up on the second ring.

I could hear the music booming in my ear, and the people were loud. Oh yeah, it's lit in there.

"You got my section ready? Me and the crew rolling through there in a few."

"Yeah, boss. I can get it ready. Listen, I'm letting you know now that the Archibald's and their crew will be here as well. Be cool tonight, Spence. I know they need their face busted in, but don't do it at 227. We cool?"

My knuckles were turning white from how hard I was gripping the phone.

"Yeah, Nardo, we cool."

"You know, I wouldn't even let them in, but you know how they do... They'll claim I only let black people in my club and not the white people, although, I have plenty of white people that roll through here. I don't need that type of heat, right now."

"It's all good," I said and hung up.

Andrew and Aaron Archibald are the thorns in my side that will never go away. Their father handed down their architect company as well. No matter how much I prove to them that my company is better, they won't back down.

Almost two hours later we were walking into the rocking Club 227. Rick dropped me off around back. My brother and his driver were in front of us. I came around the back because reporters live in front of this place. You know how many headlines some of these guys have made in the funny papers, 'Billionaire takes home sex worker' or stripper or anything they feel like making up to put in the papers. It's a gift and a curse when everyone knows who you are.

My brother and I had made it to our section to join our other friends and Selena and her sister, Joy. Along with my good friends, Elias, Omri, and Taio. I met all of them in college. Elias and Omri are fraternal twin brothers, and their father is an oil tycoon. Taio created this app called Spice It Up, which is a very successful dating app. I knew it was going to be successful and that's why I'm a silent partner on it. I have my name on a lot of shit that's going to have the grandchildren of my grandkids eating well. My grandfather's whole deal was for his family to never have to fill out an application for anybody they didn't want to. The only application I have ever filled out was my college application.

"What the hell is up?" I spoke, dapping each of my friends up.

I sat down and poured me a glass of Remy Martin and took a sip. I took my cigar out my pocket and started to fire it up while looking out across the floor. I could feel the rage inside of me growing when I looked across the floor and saw Aaron and Andrew looking directly at us. They held their drinks up like they were speaking, but I continued to glare at them.

"Don't worry about them tonight, Spence. You had a great week, and that is what we are celebrating. Okay?" Selena said to me, making me pull my eyes away from them.

I smirked and held my glass back up to them. I downed the rest of my drink and poured another glass when I stood to look down at the dancers. We normally have dancers up here, but I guess my people just wanted the atmosphere. I was scanning the floor and my eyes landed on her... her. The place was dimly lit, but I would never forget that face. Her face was much more made up than it was when I saw her earlier. Her lips were so plump and red. She was sitting with two girls and a guy. I couldn't see the two girls' faces, but I could see her and the guy. They were swaying to the music and throwing back shots. She couldn't see up here, but I still had a perfect view of her.

I pulled my phone out of my pocket and sent Nardo a text, telling him to come up here. Ten minutes later, he was walking through our door. He came and stood next to me.

"What's going on, boss?" he asked me.

He followed my eyes towards the table that I was beamed down on. I took a gulp of alcohol before I spoke.

"Is she a frequent visitor here?" I asked.

He already knew who I was talking about because he was staring at the table just like I was. There were a lot of people in that area, but that table stood out. Her beauty is so captivating. The guy must have said something funny because she burst out and started laughing. I didn't even know that she could smile because each time I had been in her presence, she had an attitude.

"She works here. That's Krimson," he said and then paused. "Why?" he asked in a much aggressive tone that I picked up on.

"Krimson is her real name?" I asked him, ignoring the tone of his voice that he had taken.

"No, and you're not going to get her real name. That's me."

"That's you, but you have her working. You have her getting naked for these guys in here, but that's you?" I questioned him while keeping my eyes on her.

"She doesn't get naked. She's a waitress."

I was going to reply, but a guy had approached the table and whispered in her ear. She waved him off and then turned back to her friends. The guy looked like he was pestering her and I was getting ready to go down there and intervene, but I saw the security guy come over there. I saw her rolling her neck and waving her hand, and then the guy escorted him away.

I felt eyes on me, and I looked across at Archibald's section and Andrew was looking me in my eyes and smirking. He must have had *something* up his sleeve. Moments later, I knew what that something was when I saw Aaron approaching their table. He leaned over and whispered in her ear and had her grinning like a school girl. The music had changed to a slow song, and he held his hand out to her, and she took it.

"That's your girl?" I chuckled.

We both watched as the pair made it to the dance floor. She had her arms around his neck, and he had his arms resting on her waist. Her attire was much different. I could see her very petite ass from here. The whole time they were dancing, he would whisper in her ear, and then he would look up at me and smile. He knew that I had my eyes on her and he had to take his chance before I could get with her. See, it's the little shit like that, that makes me want to drive my fist into his damn nose.

His frail, white ass wouldn't know what to do with all that woman. The whole time I was watching them dance, I was sipping on my drink trying to control the rage that I felt.

"That's your girl?" I repeated myself.

"Nah," he admitted. "But I want that. I'm working on it."

"Sure you are."

"She ain't gon' mess with him if that's what you are wondering. She hates rich men. She wants, as she says, a 'regular degular' guy because she works around us and she claims that we are needy, arrogant, and a whole bunch of things that I won't repeat," he said to me.

I nodded my head as I gulped the rest of my drink down. He left out the section, but I kept my eyes on them. They were on the second slow song and her back was now on his chest and she was slow grinding on him like she did have experience on the pole. The whole time she was slow grinding on him, he kept his eyes on me. I couldn't take looking at it anymore, so I took a seat and refilled my drink.

Ten minutes later, I stood up again, and saw that he was now standing at their table and it looked like she was gathering her things to leave with him. Oh, I wasn't letting that happen. I know how Aaron is with women... especially women of color. I heard that he makes them do strange shit for only a few thousand dollars. He tries to make them sign Non-Disclosure Agreements, so he won't be liable for anything, and it basically says that they agreed to do everything he wanted them to do.

Our circle was very small, but very big at the same time. The people talk. The lawsuits never see the light of day because once he figures out they went to a lawyer, he has no problem shelling out a million dollars for their silence. I'm afraid he'd do worse things to Krimson because she's feisty... and Aaron would get some type of vindication for hurting her, thinking that he's hurting me. I couldn't let anything happen to her. I *wouldn't* let anything happen to her.

Kriss

My friends had convinced me to dance with this white man, and he had now convinced me to walk with him out to his car. I had a few drinks in me, but not enough to do something stupid that I would regret in the morning. I had seen him in here a few times, but I never served him or his crew. He told me that his name was Aaron and that he had his own architect business. I thought that was dope.

When we walked outside, we walked around to the back and made it to his very lime green Lamborghini. It was a nice shiny color.

"You wanna take it for a spin?" he asked me.

"No, thank you. I can't afford to drive anything this expensive because if I wreck it, I'll have to work twelve hour days to pay for the parts."

"You won't wreck it because I'll be guiding you," he said and stepped closer to me. "What you say?" He started rubbing his bony finger down my jawline.

After not responding, he started leaning in to try and kiss me, but I stepped back. I had never been with a white guy before. I didn't see anything wrong with them, I just never had one that stepped to me the right way. Most white men who stepped to me always stepped to me saying that '*I ain't never been with a black woman before*' bullshit, which is why I never gave any one of them a chance.

"You scared to be with a white man? You think I won't be able to please you. You worried about that white men having small penises myth. I can assure you that—"

"I don't know what type of woman you think I am, but I'm not her."

"I'm sure you are; what's your price? You name it... I got it."

"Excuse me..."

"I said what's your price... five, ten, twenty thousand. I can write you a check for it right now."

Before I could even slap his ass across his face, I heard that very deep baritone voice from the elevator. He appeared next to us.

"Hey, why are you out here alone?" he asked me, not even acknowledging Aaron.

"Umm—" I started.

"Spencer," Aaron spoke through gritted teeth.

Spencer. His name is Spencer. I finally have a name with a face.

"Did you hear that, Krimson?"

I gasped at him calling me by my stage name. I guess it's not hard to get considering he did just come out of 227.

"Let me get you inside before someone harms you out here. This is no place for a woman to be out here alone. I don't want you to get kidnapped," he said and held his hand out for me to grab.

I looked at his hand, and it was either stay out here with creepy, arrogant Aaron or go with the mean bastard from the elevator. I chose the latter and placed my hand in his. We started walking away.

"Spencer, you'll be hearing from me, soon!" he yelled after us.

"Did you hear that," he asked me loud enough for Aaron to hear, making me grin like a little school girl.

We walked in silence, and as he held my hand, he was using his thumb to rub the insides of my palm. It felt so good. This is the most affection I have had in two years. He almost had me until we made it back to the front and I snatched away from him.

"What?" he questioned as if he doesn't know what he did to me earlier today.

"You closed the elevator on me! *After* I asked you to hold the elevator. What now? You want me to thank you for saving me from Aaron," I sniped.

"If you know what I know, then yes, you should be thanking me. Also, I closed the elevator on your ass because you high stepped on my freshly waxed car. You better be glad that's all my driver spat at you," he said.

My breath was caught in my throat because I didn't know what he was about to do to me. When I found my voice, I stood on my tiptoes to get as eye level with him as I could.

"Well, next time I bet your driver won't pull that big ugly ass car in the crosswalk again. Now!"

I walked away and back inside of the club, hopefully leaving all my troubles outside.

"So, how was it?" JuJu asked me when I sat back down at the table.

"How was what? How is every reaction with these raggedy ass men up in here? Trying to throw his money around to get what he wants."

"I get what you are trying to do, Kriss, but you need the money," Lawrynn said. "Feel bad later, but get the money. *Always* get the money."

"My vagina is not for sell, Lawrynn. I need the money, but selling my vagina is on the list of things that I will never do for money."

"To each its own," she said and took a big gulp of her drink.

We sat and drank for two more hours. The last thirty minutes, I gulped down two glasses of water to try and flush out this alcohol because I had to drive home. My friends left while I went to use the bathroom. After I came out, I walked to the bar to get Gene, the security guard, to walk me out to my car.

"You ready, Krimson?" he asked me.

"Kriss, can I talk to you for a second," Nardo asked me, rounding the corner.

"No, it's late, and I am tired. Maybe tomorrow," I replied. "Yes, I'm ready Gene."

He walked me outside to where I parked my car but it was not in its spot.

"Okay, I am not this drunk. I know for a fact I parked my car, right here," I said, standing in the empty parking space.

"You sure? Press the panic button on your key."

I took my keys out my bag and pushed the panic button on my keys, and I didn't hear anything.

"Somebody stole my car!" I screamed. "I drive an old ass Honda. Who the hell would want that car?" I sighed.

If it wasn't one thing, it was another.

Before I could dial the cops, the big ugly car from earlier today pulled up. The back window let down, and it was Spencer. I rolled my eyes to the sky and sighed deeply.

"Looks like you need a ride," he said. "Gene, big fella, I got this from here."

Gene started to walk away, but I grabbed his arm, begging him under my breath not to leave me out here with him. I told him that I was scared for my life with this guy. Gene assured me that I would be fine with this man and left me out there.

"No, I don't need a ride. I'll get an Uber after I call the police!" I said.

"No need to call the police. I can take you to your car if you get in."

"You stole my car? How did you know that was my car?"

"Not exactly."

"Unless there are two definitions of stealing, then..."

My sentence was cut short when he opened the door. He walked swiftly over to me and towered over me. I took a step back because I didn't want to break my neck looking up at him.

"Krim, you should get in the car," he ordered me like I was a child.

"No, I don't know you. My dad always told me not to get in the car with strangers."

He sighed. He didn't say another word. He picked me up and threw me over me his shoulder and walked me back to his car. He slammed me in the car, scooted me over, and then got in and shut the door. I looked ahead and saw the man who called me out of my name.

"I should jump over this seat and start whamming on your head for calling me a whore," I snapped at the driver.

"Can you roll that up, please?" Spencer said to the driver.

The driver nodded his head, and the deeply tinted glass started to slowly roll up. Once the glass was completely up, he turned his body towards me and just stared at me.

"Do you know who I am?"

"Spencer," I said, remembering his name from our earlier encounter.

"Yes, Spencer is my last name. My name is Travis Spencer the Third."

"Ooookkkk," I dragged out as I looked at him with a confused look on my face.

"Does my name ring a bell?"

"No, it doesn't. Why are you asking me these questions? Am I supposed to know who you are or something, my God! Are you so used to ladies knowing who you are, throwing themselves at you, and the first one that doesn't know who you are, you steal their cars and kidnap them?" I sniped.

I hated guys in Atlanta with a little clout because they swear up and down that everyone knows who they are, and you are dumb little bird if you don't know who they are.

"Your mouth is so damn smart. Why do you always got something smart to say? I just wanted to know your name, and why were you in my building today?"

"Your building? Ground-Up?" I asked with a shocked look on my face.

He looked and smelled like money, but I didn't know the significance of it.

"Yes, I am the CEO of Ground-Up. Now again, why were you in my building giving me attitude?"

"NO. I won't tell you! Please take me to my car, NOW!"

The rest of the ride was quiet until we pulled into a vacant parking lot. There was my Honda, safe and sound. The car was barely in park before I jumped out of the car and jumped in mine. I could have told him that my dad works there, but I was not going to subject my dad to any bullying from that man. I sped home and took a very hot shower and dived into my sheets.

Spence

I was laying in the bed twirling her license in my fingers. "Kriss Brown," I read aloud.

She was in such a rush to get out of my car that she dropped her wallet in the back seat of my car. Of course, I went through it and saw that she had every type of credit card that you can ever imagine, except an AMEX or Black Card. Her car was easy to find because she had a purple car tag in front of her car that said 'Krim' on it. I wanted to talk to her more, and she completely shut down on me when I asked her why was she in my building. When she rushed out of my car, I couldn't help but to notice how good her bottom looked in that jogging suit she had on. She was so interesting, and what made her even more interesting was when I told her who I was and she had a stunned look on her face. Either she is a great actor, or she really doesn't know who I am.

"Twenty-seven years old."

I promised myself and my brother that I wouldn't mess with another young girl, but Kriss was just too intriguing not to. I looked at her information card in her wallet, and it was filled out completely. I honestly didn't know that people filled these things out. I grabbed my phone and called her. I'm not sure if I was going to say anything. I just wanted to hear her voice. I'm sure she was sleeping.

"Who is this calling me this late?" she answered groggily into the phone.

I didn't say anything. She was breathing heavily into the phone like she was falling asleep while holding the phone.

"Malcolm, is that you?" she asked into the phone.

Not saying anything, I wanted to see if she would say something else.

"Malcolm, if this is you, I would like for you to stop calling me from different numbers. You made your choice. Now get a life and stop dialing my number," she growled and hung up the phone.

Malcolm had to have been the guy that hardened her heart. I wondered who he was. I grabbed her wallet off the night stand and started digging through it some more to see if I could get a last name on this Malcolm guy, but there was nothing. I wanted to call her back just to hear her voice again, but I didn't want to seem like a creep. After thinking about it some more, I called her back.

"Hello! Malcolm, what did I just tell you?" she snapped into the phone.

"Kriss," I called her name with a stern voice.

"H-hello. Who is this?" she whispered into the phone.

"I think you know who this is, Kriss... Kriss Brown."

Click.

I looked at the phone, and she had hung up on me. I chuckled because I was going to enjoy breaking her little black ass down and have her groveling at my feet. I put her things on my nightstand and went to sleep.

The Next Day

After I had finished my two-hour work-out, I got in the shower. When I got out, I wrapped a towel around me and walked back into my room to see my stylist, Jaquel, standing there looking at me with a crazy look on her face. Jaquel was Zahara's sister.

"Why are you looking at me like that? Am I supposed to be somewhere today, or something?" I asked.

"Um, yes, you are supposed to be—wow," Zahara said, walking into the room and cutting her statement off when she saw my wet body wrapped in my towel. "Wow, Jah always said your body was nice, but I didn't know it was *this* nice," she chuckled.

"Chill, Zahara. Where am I supposed to be and when?"

"Well, you are acting like you are not one of Atlanta's Most Eligible Bachelors for the eighth year in a row. You have the shoot in about an hour."

"Oh damn, I completely forgot about that. Thank y'all for reminding me."

"Yeah, I'll be downstairs with Rick flirting with him, while you and Jaquel up here trying to get you done up," Zahara said and walked out the room.

Zahara was pairing up outfits while I grabbed some briefs and walked into the bathroom to moisturize and put on my briefs. After I was done, I walked back out and Jaquel was standing there with a perplexed look on her face.

"You're forty now and I want to try something different for this magazine shoot. What you think? You wanna do a blazer and some slim jeans, or maybe a really tailored suit that's above the ankles? You know that new trend that the young guys—"

"Jah, the first thing you said should have told you that I am not with the over the ankle tailored pants. I'm forty and I don't like my ankles being shown. My pants are tailored just fine already."

Sucking her teeth and sighing, she gave me the charcoal gray Dolce and Gabbana suit to put on. I'm sure that I was going to change at least two or three times before the shoot was over.

After I got dressed, Jaquel had my other outfit changes in bags, taking them downstairs to put them in the truck.

"Before you get there, I just wanna let you know that both Archibald brothers will be there. Don't act a fool, ok?" Zahara said as soon as we were in the truck.

"I can't get away from those dudes man. I had to save some girl from Aaron's ass last night."

"Some girl?" Jaquel asked with her eyebrows almost touching the roof of the car.

"Yeah, you know who she is," Zahara smirked, cosigning her sister's surprised look.

"I don't, but you will though by the time this shoot is over," I told Zahara, handing her Kriss's ID. "Find out everything you know about this girl. When I say everything... I mean everything. Down to the medical records, financial records, and all that. I need everything."

"Sir, that is at least two days' work," Zahara said.

"Not for the top-flight assistant of the world. I'm going to my office after this. Have Rick take you anywhere you need to go while Jaquel's in here making me look like a black King," I said as soon as the truck pulled up to the place where the photo shoot is going to take place.

"But—" Zahara spoke.

"But nothing... thank you for everything that you do."

Both Jaquel and I climbed out the truck, leaving Zahara sitting in there with a shocked look on her face.

"I'll call Rick when I'm ready."

I shut the door, and Rick pulled off. Jah and I walked into the building and my eyes automatically landed on those white ass Archibald brothers. I smiled at them both, so they wouldn't know they made my skin crawl every time I was in the same vicinity.

"Mr. Spencer, we're waiting for you," the photographer came over to us and said. "My name is Mickie Green," she introduced herself to myself and Jaquel.

"Spence is fine," I corrected her.

We followed the photographer in the room where it was a couple of background sheets and a changing space. The lights were bright as the sun, and I knew I was going to get hot soon. Honestly, I hated taking pictures. I only took pictures for family pictures and this stupid Atlanta bachelor shit. This shit right here always brings the ladies my way in abundance. Not that I needed help getting the ladies anyway, it's just that when they see my picture in the magazine they be swarming in like birds when it is migration time.

"Spence, can you stand right here. We are going to take a few pictures of you standing this way, and then a few with you smiling—"

"No smiling," I cut her off.

"But your smile... never mind."

She took a few snaps of me in several different poses and on several different backgrounds. I changed into a different outfit and took more photos. My forehead started to sweat and the make-up artist came and dabbed at my forehead so I could finish the shoot. My portion of the shoot was over in an hour and a half.

"Don't go anywhere; we have to get a picture with all of y'all together. Did you bring a black tux, Spence?" Mickie asked me as I was getting ready to leave the room.

"Yes, we do have it," Jaquel answered for me. "You might as well get changed into it now, Spence," she directed at me.

Following her orders, I went behind the curtain and changed into my black tux. We walked back out into the room where the other men were waiting and took a seat.

"So, the girl you wanted my sister to look up. Is she going to be your new girl?" Jaquel said.

"Nah. I just wanted to know more about her. The encounters that I had with her... intrigue me."

"*Intrigue,* huh?" she queried with such sarcasm in her voice.

"Don't do this, Jaquel. Not here. Not now. We had what we had, and now it's finished. You were able to keep your job because you said that you were cool."

"Spence, I'm sorry. I just... I shouldn't have said anything. I'm okay," she said and shook her head as if she was shaking away any thoughts of us.

Jaquel and I were good friends. We still are in my eyes. One night, we were at 227 and I had one too many Patron shots, and Jah started looking good as hell. I guess she had one too many shots as well and next thing you know, we were in the back of my truck having sex. We were both drunk. After that, we had sex a few more times, and then she asked me to take her on a date and I had to slow things down quickly because I didn't look at her like that. We never had sex again because I didn't want to blur the lines between us. Even after we stopped having sex, she still hints at us being together, but I block it.

"Okay, rich and handsome men, it is timmmeeee for the group photo. Gather around," Mickie came out of the room and sang before I could respond to Jaquel's apology. I told her to call Rick and tell him that we were ready, so I wouldn't have to stand around when this was over.

We all gathered around so we could take the photo. I was one of the taller ones so I was in the back. Aaron and Andrew were the same height as me so they came and stood on either side of me.

"Mr. Save a Hoe," Aaron said and chuckled.

"Yeah, saving *her* from a hoe," I whispered and smirked.

He wanted to say something else, but Mickie had told us to smile. After the photo shoot was over, Rick was outside waiting. We got in the truck and Zahara was sitting there with a huge manila folder full of papers. A huge smile spread across my face because I knew that Zahara would get it done.

"You better be glad that I love you, Spence," she grinned and handed me the folder.

My fingers were itching to open the folder, but I wanted to wait until I made it to my office. The tapping of my fingers was the only noise in the car. I kept looking out of the window to force myself not to open the folder.

Thirty minutes later, Rick was pulling around the back of my building.

"Rick, I won't be up here long. I'll call you," I said to him and he nodded his head.

Up in my office, I was going through the folder and I saw that she had a clean bill of health. She has two degrees and she's smart as hell. Made the Chancellor's list every year she was in school. She was a tutor at Spelman and all of that. My preconceived notion of her was all wrong. I felt stupid reading her files. I see that she has been trying to get away from 227 but no one was hiring her because of her bad ass credit. I found out that it was her dad, Charlie Brown, who worked for me. He was a janitor that has been here for years, and I can't believe that I never noticed him. Now, I felt like shit and very entitled.

After I finished reading her file, I placed her file in my briefcase, and I got started on my work. I smirked to myself because Kriss Brown was going to be mine... at least for one night.

Kriss

*A*ll today I had been lounging around the house in my pajamas. Since I work at night, I normally lounge around all day unless I have something to do. Every time my phone rang, chirped, or anything, I jumped, thinking that it was Spence. If he could have my car towed, then I'm sure that it was just as easy to get my phone number. I know for a fact that Nardo's hating ass didn't give it to him. In his eyes, I am his, and nobody else can have me. Some of the girls have told me that he be cock blocking me with some of those guys that work there. I don't care to be honest because those rich guys are just not my cup of tea.

I went downstairs to see that my dad was sitting at the table reading the paper. I don't know how I'm going to tell him that he may lose his job because of me.

"You okay? You look a little flustered," my dad spoke, not even looking over the paper.

"Dad," I sighed, and pulled the chair from under the table and sat in it. "I have something that I need to tell you."

He closed the paper, giving me his undivided attention.

"Yes, pumpkin," he said, calling me by my childhood nickname.

"I think I may have gotten you fired from your job at Ground-Up. I didn't mean to... I just..."

"How? What do you mean?" he queried.

"Well, I had a couple of unfortunate encounters with the boss and I must say that they aren't pretty. I cursed him out a couple of times and I shouldn't have let my anger get the—"

"Ssshhh, pumpkin. I haven't been fired yet and I probably won't be fired. I worked for Spence's father and trust me; my job is very secure there. Also, how did you encounter him and why were they unfortunate?"

"He just... ugh, I don't know."

"Crush? Maybe?"

"God, no, Dad! You know I will never date a man with that much money. They think they can run over you, have multiple women, and just do whatever it is that they want to do and think that they are not supposed to have any consequences, ya know? They are so arrogant, and I will not be someone's trophy wife."

"But you are a trophy though. Any man that makes it to putting that ring on your finger will have to work damn hard to get you and will be very appreciative of you. That's how I view trophies. Something or *someone* I worked hard to get and something I never took for granted," he said and winked at me. "But, no need to fret, darling, I assure you that I have not lost my job."

My heart slowed back to normal when he assured me for the second time that he hadn't lost his job. I got up and kissed him on his forehead and then went to make me a protein shake. After I finished putting all my ingredients in my shake, I chuckled to myself when I thought about telling Spence that I would grind his heart up in my shake, knowing that was not physically possible... well, unless you're into that type of thing.

After drinking my shake, I went back up to my bedroom and got in the bed. I looked at my phone and had two missed phone calls. One from Lawrynn and one from the number that Spence called me from last night. I wasn't calling Spence back, but I definitely had to call Lawrynn back.

"What's good?" she picked up on the first ring. "Why you ain't answer the first time I called you?"

"I was downstairs talking to my dad. Listen, why did Spence call me during the 'legs open' hours. I don't even know how he got my number."

"You need to get laid, Kriss. It's been two years. Every dude ain't Malcolm, damn."

"Girl, you know I don't just give my kitty to anyone. I'm not *you*."

She laughed so loud before replying, "You need to be *me*... at least once, chile. Ain't no harm in having a couple of one night stands. These dudes do it... all the time and with no regards to these women feelings. Gotta start treating them how they treat you and you should have done that with Malcolm, but you were too weak. You had a chance to get back at him with his best friend... the one he sees as his brother, and you took the high road. I would have ridden that thang into the sunset."

"I'm sure you would have," I chuckled. "I'll end up having a one night stand and find myself in a whole one sided relationship. I just can't do that to myself. You know how I am," I sighed.

"You're right. I don't think you're able to have sex without catching feelings. You're right, don't. Anyways, I was calling you to let you know that I'm falling through 227 tonight. I think Russ said he had some shit to do. So, how long are you working tonight?"

"Girl, as short as possible. I'm already annoyed to the highest level. So, I'll see you tonight," I said and hung up the phone.

I fell back against the bed and sighed. Malcolm Arisma. Malcolm Arisma was my first everything. He transferred to my school in high school and I was the first girl he had eyes for. His smooth, peanut butter skin and long, sandy red dreads had me hot in the middle the first time I saw him. I never would have thought that he was Haitian until he spoke with that deep Haitian accent... one you couldn't fake. He approached me and told me that I was one of the cutest girls that he had ever seen in his life, and that was all that he had to say to spin me into his web. Malcolm was so tall and stocky, that I couldn't resist him when he asked me out on a date.

After our first date, it was really murder she wrote. We were inseparable. Things didn't change until after I let him take my virginity. It was like he became a different person to me, but I was so in love that I took every excuse as to why he said he changed. We were on and off in high school and college. I would break up with him when he would piss me off, and then he would come bearing gifts and making googly eyes at me, instantly melting my insides. We did that all the way up until I was twenty-five.

I will always remember my twenty-fifth birthday as the worst birthday anyone can have on earth. The day of my twenty-fifth birthday, Malcolm called me early that morning and told me that he wanted to pamper me all day to get ready for the night that he had set up for me. Immediately after that phone call, my email buzzed with a receipt to go to Elite Day Spa to be pampered. I got a facial, a mani and pedi, and a two-hour massage. After that, he transferred five hundred dollars to my account to go get me an outfit to wear for our date. After I had done all of that, I came home, took a shower, and beat my face to capacity, although I don't have to wear much. I was looking so good, I knew that Malcolm was going to get me pregnant. He told me that he was going to pick me up at seven.

Seven thirty had rolled around and he hadn't picked me up, so I went over to his house. I always had a key to his place. I stuck my key into the lock and pushed the door open. The pungent odor of fish and weed soiled the air in the foyer. My stomach turned at the thought of what I was getting ready to walk in on. I walked into the living room and my heart dropped to my feet at the sight of Malcolm laid out on the couch naked, with a woman's head between his legs. They were both sleep after what had to be an intense round of sex... or several... who knows?

At the time, I wasn't good with confrontation, so I wasn't going to say anything. I left the key on the arm of the couch by his head, so he would know that I had been there, and quietly backed out of the house. I drove like a mad woman through the streets with tears streaming down my eyes. I didn't want to call Lawrynn to hear the 'I told you so's.' I didn't want to call Russ because Russ would beat his ass, which he needed, but I knew that Malcolm had a gun, and I didn't want to risk his life.

When I made it back home, my make-up was all cried off. I was thankful that my dad was in his room, so I wouldn't have to explain why I was back so early. Malcolm never did call me, but he did call me the next afternoon and told me that he was so sorry and that he had been in a car accident and he was passed out from the meds that they put him on. I was so appalled at how the lie rolled off his tongue, that I laughed a hearty laugh in his ear. I had to let him know that I put the key on the couch, so I was there. I was so pissed that he insulted my intelligence that I wanted to beat his ass. He promised to make it up to me and even transferred a thousand dollars in my account to prove how sorry he was. I hung up on him and that was the last time we ever spoke... voluntarily.

He stalked me for a while before he ended up giving up. Every few months that he thinks I have moved on, he'll make a new number and text me to let me know that he still loves me and he thinks that we could work out, but nah. There was no going back after that, and he should have known that. I deleted his ass off every social media app I had him on, which helped me get over him. Also, Atlanta is huge and it was 'out of sight, out of mind' that also helped me get over him. I stopped hanging around the places that I knew he would be.

That is why when Spence called me, I thought that it was Malcolm because I hadn't heard from him in a few months. I looked at the time to see how much time I had to nap before I had to be at work. I had a good three hours to nap before I had to get up. I was already ready to clock out and I hadn't even clocked in yet. I knew that I was going to be cranky as hell tonight and just because I was cranky, those stupid men were going to be extra annoying.

Later that night...

I was staring at the mirror and rolling my neck around so I could relax. I had on a red corset with a pair of red, lace cheeky panties paired with a black garter belt set and a pair of black Kate Spade glitter shoes made like those white Keds. I didn't feel like putting on heels. I walked out of the room and onto the floor, and it was jumping in here and it was only midnight. I could tell that it was going to be a long night but... a good tip night.

"Hey, baby!" Miguel spoke to me. "You are just in time. I need you to take these bottles to section seven. Just a warning, it's Aaron and his brother. Please let Nardo know if they say some out of the way shit to you. They are close to getting their privileges revoked after the way they talked to Tya before you got here."

"What they say to her?" I asked.

"One of those bitches they are with in that section made Tya trip and she dropped one of the Floyd Mayweather Tequila bottles."

"Yikes!" I hissed.

"Right, you know it cost fifteen hundred dollars, but after they made her trip, they yelled expletives that I won't repeat and the poor girl ran away crying. It didn't help that Nardo got onto her as well. It was a mess, but I will say that Nardo checked those Archibald's for calling her out of her name and gave him two bottles of the Tequila on the house, but you know Tya has to replace that bottle from her tips or whatever, but you ain't hear all of that from me."

"Give me these damn bottles, and I wish one of those girls would try me. It will be smoke in the city."

Miguel laughed when I took the bottles away from him. I trucked over to their section and soon as I walked in, I saw the white girl's foot come out. I stepped over her foot and I got directly in front of her and she immediately recoiled, just like I knew she would.

"You listen to me, I am not the one. You stick your foot out in front of me and you will only pull back an ankle. I'm not the one and you're too damn old to be playing childish games, and for what? Now, I will be your server for the rest of the night and I will let you know that I am about that action," I snapped at her, and her face immediately turned red. I turned and faced the rest of the section who had had their lips together. "And that goes to anybody in this section. You got the right server tonight."

I set the bottles down on the table and started to walk out of the section, but I heard clapping, prompting me to turn around to see that it was Aaron, who had a smirk on his face.

"I knew it was a reason that I liked you, Krimson. Your buddy's not here to save you tonight, so when you get off come to my section and let a real man show you how to be treated," he said.

"And you the real man?" I questioned before walking out, making sure to eye the girl that stuck her foot out.

As soon as I got back to the bar, Miguel had a whole tray of bottles waiting for me.

"VIP room ten," he said.

"How many people are in that damn room?"

"I don't know. I'm not even sure who is back there, but I know your tip is about to be crazy big. Their bill already at a hundred thousand.

Your tip about to be at least ten thousand, depending on how they tip."

"I hope so, so I can get that bottle for Tya. You know she is trying to help her parents out as much as she can, ya know. Fifteen hundred dollars will hurt her pockets deeply."

"Your heart is so good, Krimson. You deserve the world," he said, making me smile at him.

I grabbed the tray of bottles, praying that no one bumped into me. The sections in this club are low-key anyway, but the VIP rooms are real low-key. You can only get into them by coming in through the back way. They have a small table kiosk that you can order the drinks from and they can choose a waitress of their choice to bring the bottles. I'm used to getting chose, so I wasn't sure who could be in there. I'm just happy about this tip that I'm about to get.

I finally made my way through the crowd and pushed the door open. There were a bunch of fine ass men... black men... that started hooting and hollering the minute I bent over and set the tray on the table. They should have been hollering at the women that were in there dancing for them. After I set the tray on the table, I looked up to see *him* sitting deep in the corner by himself. He used his index finger to beckon me over to him. I slightly shook my head no, and he shook his head yeah. When he stood up, I started slowly backing up towards the door.

His strides were quicker than my baby steps and before I could open the door, he wrapped his arm around my waist and pulled me into him. My head went right into his chest. He lifted me an inch off the floor and walked back to the spot where he was sitting. I was so intoxicated by his smell that I didn't even realize that he had sat me on my feet. He kept his arm wrapped around my waist and I was standing in between his legs.

"Who is Malcolm?" was the first thing he asked, ruining the fairytale moment I was having.

I tried to pry his arm away from around my waist, but he tightened the grip.

"You ruined the moment by asking me about my ex."

"Well, you called me his name on the phone, several times, so I was wondering who he was."

"I have to get back to work, Spence," I said and tried to free myself from his grip again, making him pull me tighter...into his crotch.

"No, you don't. You're mine... my waitress for tonight."

"What?"

"I gave Nardo the money—"

"I don't have sex for money. So, you might as well get your money back," I said, rolling my neck.

"Who said you did? You must do," he said in a smart tone.

"I'm out of here," I growled, digging my nails into skin, making his arm fall.

I tried to walk away, but he grabbed me by garter belt, stopping me. He pulled me through the door of the small bedroom that is in the VIP room. He locked the door behind him. When he let me go, I walked away from him, but he stood by the door. He must have known that I was going to try and make a break for it the minute he walked away from the door. While he was looking at his arm, I took him in.

He had on a pair of tailored navy pants with a lilac colored button down which was not all the way buttoned up. I never knew that the color lilac could look so damn good on a man. I could see that he had on two small but noticeable gold rope chains paired with a gold bracelet on his arm and gold diamonds in his ear. His hair was cut low and his beard and mustache was lined to perfection, as if he just got out of the barber's chair a few hours ago. His lips were so thick... can you describe lips as thick? I don't know, but that's what his are. Even though it's dark in here, I can tell that his skin was perfect. The way his muscles bulged from under that shirt made my mouth water. Is this really what black billionaires look like? Honestly, I always pictured black billionaires giving off Bill Gates vibes.

"So, now that you've salivated over me for the last couple of minutes, do you like what you see?" he asked. "Come here, Krimson. I have something that you might need," he said.

"And... and what is that?" I spoke, barely above the music that was playing.

"Come see," he said while beckoning me over with that index finger that I wouldn't mind him pushing inside of me.

I shook away the nasty thought as I walked slowly to him. I stood almost a foot away from him, making him reach out to grab me by the string of my thong, pulling me closer to him. I was so close to him that not even a piece of paper could get between us. I didn't want to look up at him, so I kept my vision on his chest.

"Look up at me, Krimson," he whispered.

I shook my head profusely. I hadn't been this close to a man in a couple of years and I was getting excited...which was not good because I had on cheeky panties, and when I get excited... I get excited. My essence could literally fill up a cup, and I didn't bring a change of underwear.

He gripped my chin between his index and thumb and lifted my head up to him. I thought that he was going to kiss me. Hell, I wanted him to kiss me. I was so nervous that I couldn't look him in his eyes. My eyes darted from side to side to avoid looking him in his face. He slid his hand in his back pocket and he pulled a card out of it, and I saw that it was my ID.

"How did you get that?"

"I have your wallet. You dropped it when you rushed out of my car. Tell me, Krimson, why are you shaking? Are you afraid of me?"

I nodded my head up and down and his eyebrows raised in confusion.

"Why?"

"I was afraid that if I didn't do whatever you asked me to do, my dad would lose his job. I'm afraid because I haven't been this close to a man in years and it's... intimidating. Very."

"I'm not that type of guy, Krimson, and I will never do anything to a woman without her consent. What do you want to do?"

"What... what you mean?" I stuttered as I darted my eyes back to his chest.

"Keep your eyes on me," he said, making me look back up at him.

"I can smell you... her. Are you excited? Excited to be around me."

I nodded my head slowly.

Leaning over, he whispered in my ear, "Can I touch you?"

"Where?" flew out of my mouth like I wasn't nervous that I was in here with this man.

All I could hear was Lawrynn's voice in my head telling me to live a little, but I was chickening out.

"Here," he said and rubbed that index finger up and down my jawline. "And here." He rubbed his finger across my lips. "Also here." He rubbed his hand up my thigh and I grabbed his hand when he neared my throbbing middle.

"I'm so embarrassed right now," I said. "I have to go," I said and tried to walk out, but he blocked me.

"Why are you embarrassed? Look at me."

"I don't know you, ok! I don't know you and I am lusting over you. I feel... I have never felt like this before," I admitted. "I'm scared, Spence. I can't do anything with you because I know that I am just a disposable to you. I don't want to be that to you, or any man. I don't care about money. Can you please let me out?" I begged before he wore me down.

"What if I told you that I won't treat you like a disposable? What if I told you that I just wanted to taste you? Stick my fingers inside of you and then taste you. That's it."

"That's it?"

"You have my word," he said and raised his right hand in the air.

Just as he did that "You Remind me of Something" by R. Kelly started playing, and I knew that JuJu was about to go on stage and kill it. I usually watch her sets, but I'm stuck in here... with this man. This fine man who only wants to stick his fingers inside of me. We both bobbed our head to the music and smiled at each other on certain parts.

"Satisfaction... Guaranteed," he sang along with Robert.

He slid my ID back in his pocket and used that as an opportunity to slide his hand up my thigh. My juices had now saturated the seat of my panties and were coming out of the sides, sticking to my leg. He rubbed his finger up and down my bikini line and his eyes got large when he felt how sticky it was.

"Wow," he whispered. "Can I touch you? Please?" he pleaded.

I nodded my head up and down.

"No, say it! Say, Spence, you can touch me," he groaned, impatiently, as he continued to rub his finger up and down my bikini line.

"Spence, you can touch me," I granted him the permission he so desperately wanted.

You would think after I gave him permission to touch me, he would have rushed to push his finger inside of me, but he didn't.

"Krimson, can I taste you... with my tongue? Please? You don't even have to take your panties off."

Reluctantly, I said, "Yes, Spence, you can taste me with your tongue."

He got on his knees and started placing kisses on my thighs. I looked down at him as he gave the seat of my panties a long sniff. I had never had that happen before.

"God," he moaned before placing his forehead on my mound as if he needed to catch his breath.

From that very position, he snaked his tongue out of his mouth and used the tip of his tongue to flick at my engorged bud. After he flicked his tongue out of his mouth a few times, he went down and caught it between his teeth and bit down softly and continued to flick his tongue over it at the same time.

"My god," I whispered, and placed my hand on the back of his head.

Who knew getting orally pleased with your panties on would feel this good. He grabbed my cheeks and caressed them while he focused on my bud. He increased the pressure and as he increased the pressure, my breaths started to quicken. I held my head back as I continued to pant and moan. I was starting to see stars and he knew it because he never let up.

"Speennnceee," I cried out as a wave of pleasure came over me.

My knees got weak and I was getting ready to fall. He was so strong because I was now damn near sitting on his hands while he continued his assault. I couldn't take it anymore and I moved his head back. His chest was rising and falling like he had just had the same orgasm as me. I tried to stand up, but my legs were still weak. If he could do me like that in a matter of minutes, there is no way that I would last with flesh on flesh.

Spence

Krimson and I stared at each other as we were both trying to catch our breath. I was slowly losing my breath as I tried to suck the life out of her. Her panties were saturated with her juices so I got a small glimpse of how she tasted. I couldn't wait to push my tongue in her hole, but I was going to wait until she wanted it. I could tell that she was blushing. The heat that was radiating off her skin had me wanted to dive on her.

"Say something," I managed to say.

"That felt... felt amazing," she whispered.

"There's more where that came from. I'll let the next moves be up to you, baby girl. No pressure," I said to her.

I stood up and helped her to her feet. In one swift movement, she pushed me back against the door very aggressively. She tried to place her lips on mine but I moved, making her cower away, in embarrassment.

"Oh my god! I'm so sorry, I shouldn't have—"

I placed my finger over her lips, making her hush and fold her lips into her mouth.

"Krimson, treating you as a disposable would be to have my way with you in this club. You're better than this. I need you in my bed... if that's where you want to go."

She nodded her slowly, but that wasn't fast enough for me. She was unsure. I didn't want her to wake up and regret anything with me.

"Baby girl, I need you to be sure. I don't want you to wake up and regret your actions. I know you're scared, but I promise you I won't do anything you don't want to do. If at any moment, you step foot into my home and you want to leave, I promise, you will be free to go."

"Spence, I want to leave with you," she said with much more certainty in her voice.

"Good. I'll be around back when you gather your things... and I'll cash out the ticket, so you can get your tip. Hurry up too, Krimson, because I can't wait to get you to my home. I can't wait to get you out of your clothes and treat you how your body has never been treated before. She smiled at me.

"I'm embarrassed. I can't walk out of here with wet thighs and panties," she said.

I walked out of the room and came back with my blazer. She put it on and it instantly swallowed her up. She walked out of the room and my brother and some of the other men were too busy receiving head, that they didn't even notice Krimson walk out. Luckily, I rode by myself so after I cashed the kiosk out, I walked out back to the car.

Earlier, after reading the extensive file on her, I couldn't wait to get finished with my work for today. I came here with the intentions of seeing her. I didn't think that I would be so bold as to corner her like that, but I felt like it was now or never. I was shocked that she would think that I would fire her father over her not talking to me. I wonder if she told him about our encounters. If she did, he would probably come find me so we could have a chat. Monday was probably going to be real interesting.

I licked my lips to see if I could taste her still. I couldn't taste her, but I could smell her on my upper lip. She smelled so good, I swear I wanted to keep those panties that she had on tonight for a couple of days to get a whiff of them. I couldn't wait to push my tongue inside of her because she needed it. I looked at my watch to see that I had been waiting for her for almost twenty minutes. My high was starting to leave. I hoped that she hadn't changed her mind but if she did, I couldn't do anything about it because I wasn't going to force her to do anything that she didn't want to do.

After waiting for fifteen more minutes, I was getting ready to call her, but I saw her walking out with the security guy. He escorted her all the way to my car and the minute she got in the car, I could see the puffiness in her eyes.

"Krimson, what's wrong? I don't want to force—"

"It's not you, Spence. It's Nardo! I walked back into the dressing room to get dressed and he came in there to bring me my tip—thank you by the way— and he started laughing at me talking about *'everybody had a price. I knew you had a price, Kriss,'*" she said in his thick accent. "I don't want the reputation of having sex for money."

"Baby girl. Look at me."

She whipped her head around towards me ready to say something smart.

"Have I offered you any money?"

"No," she whispered.

"Have you ever left with another man?"

"No."

"Okay then. You can't control what other people think of you," I said to her and drove out of the parking lot.

After a few moments of silence, she spoke.

"Sounds like something a rich person would say," she said and laughed. "How rich are you anyway?"

"I don't normally discuss my finances with people but since it's you, I'll tell you, but if I had to guess, I'll say 2.3 including everything my name is on."

"Billion dollars. 2.3 billion dollars. What do you do with that much money? You'll never spend that much money in your lifetime."

"Ehhh, my grandfather wanted to make sure that none of his family would ever have to fill out an application for anyone else, and I plan on carrying out that legacy and hoping that the Spencer family will go in history books."

"Have you ever thought about what would you do if your kids don't want to learn how to build buildings or something like that? What if your daughter wants to be the next Madam CJ Walker or your son wants to be the next Gordon Ramsey, do you force a pencil in their hand making them draw or what?" she questioned.

"I don't have kids, so I haven't thought that far. I don't plan on having kids, so hopefully my brother or sister have kids that want to take over the business or at least learn how to so they can teach someone else how to. Let's not talk about that right now. Let's just focus on the task at hand," I said, wanting to change the subject.

Bringing up a hypothetical son that wanted to be a chef struck a chord with me because I wanted to be the next Gordon Ramsay, but my dad took the utensils out of my hand and put a pencil there. There was an awkward silence before she placed her soft hand on my hand which was laying on the gear shift.

"I'm so sorry, Travis," she whispered.

Hearing her call me Travis sent chills down my spine and into my toes. I don't ever want her to call me Spence again after hearing Travis roll off her lips. I didn't ask her for what, I just looked at her, hoping that she would continue.

"You didn't want to be an architect, did you?" she asked.

I shook my head 'no.' I was shocked that I had even answered this question because I had never admitted this out loud to anyone. I was waiting for her response.

"I'm sorry, again. Are you happy with your life right now? Being an architect?"

"I mean... yeah, I am. I make good money. I can come and go as I please. I'm single with no kids and I looked damn good to be forty—"

"FORTY!" she screamed.

I pulled up to my gate and stopped. If my age was going to be a problem to her, I wasn't going to type my code into this gate, and I was going to turn around and take her back to her car.

"Is my age a problem?" I asked, slightly offended.

"N-no... I just... you don't look... how are you forty?" she stuttered.

"Because my mother had me forty years ago. That's how I'm forty."

I typed my code into the gate and drove up the cobblestone driveway. My ten thousand square foot, ten bedrooms, and eleven-bathroom house always made people's mouths drop. Of course, I designed it myself. I had the regular stuff like a pool, gym, man cave, movie room, and all the bells and whistles.

"So much house," she whispered to herself. "You're not afraid to live here alone?" she queried.

"No. My house is well protected. You can't even get close to my property without the cameras in my home popping on."

She didn't say anything. I parked the car and went around the other side to open the door for her. I handed her the wallet she left in my car the moment she stepped out. I grabbed her bag for her and led her into my house. When I opened the door, she grabbed her heart and fell backwards against the door.

"You don't have a roof? How don't you have a roof?!"

"I have a roof, it's just glass. Really, really, really thick glass, so trust me, you could shoot at the glass with twenty machine guns in the same spot and it wouldn't even chip the glass. I love a moonlit house. When the sun is shining bright, it shades. You know how your glasses do when you walk in the sunlight."

"Holy smokes! I can't breathe. This house is so wonderful. Oh my God!"

Her reaction is so authentic and it made me smile.

"The gray and yellow color scheme is giving me such a vibe. I can't get over how beautiful this house is. I'm sure you had an interior designer to decorate this. Do you collect art? I have so many questions about everything," she spoke while clasping her hands together like she was a realtor who had come up on a sale.

"Yes, I had an interior designer. No, I don't collect art. My parents and my brother do. I collect other things," I said.

"Other things like what?"

"Would you like a drink to calm your nerves, Kriss? I'll give you a tour, but I don't want you to have a heart attack before we get finished with the whole house."

"Yes, please. Sangria?"

I pulled her into the kitchen and pulled out a glass to pour her some Sangria. Luckily, Sangria is my favorite type of drink I use to unwind after an easy day. I handed her the glass and started giving her the tour. She kicked her shoes off, I'm assuming to get a feel for the plush carpets, which felt like you were walking on clouds. I took her out back to show her my car collection.

"How much is this worth?" she asked as she stared out at my fleet of cars.

I had so many cars... old and new.

"I lost count at a hundred million," I said.

Her mouth formed into an 'O' and when she didn't say anything, I led her away. I noticed that when we were halfway done with the tour, her mood had changed.

"Everything, okay?" I asked her.

"Yes. Yes. I just… this damn house. It's so perfect," she whispered.

We were outside my bedroom door.

"You ready for the main attraction, baby girl?" I asked her.

She bit her lip and nodded her head up and down slowly. I opened the door and I got the same authentic reaction that I got at the front door.

"My whole house can fit in this room. What's through the door?"

"The closet."

I watched her as she walked across the floor to my closet. Her body is so beautiful. She had on a red jumpsuit and her hair was in the big, thick curls that I liked so much. I couldn't wait to rub my fingers through her hair just to feel how soft it is. After a few minutes, she walked back out and started shaking her head.

"If you were to sell this house, how much would you sell it for?" she queried.

"I don't ever plan on selling it. Not ever. It will forever be in the Spencer family," I said.

There was an awkward silence and she took the last sip of her drink and placed it on my drawer. We stared at each other. I guess we were waiting to see who would make the first move. I beckoned for her to come over to me and she shook her head no, and I nodded my head yes.

"Come here, Kriss," I spoke softly.

She walked slowly over to me and stood directly in front of me. I started unbuttoning her jumpsuit and her labored breath was turning me on. I slid her jumpsuit off her shoulders, making sure to graze her skin until it was all the way off. She was now standing in front of me in the sexiest black lace bra with no panties on. I planned to take my time with this woman.

$\mathcal{K}riss$

$\mathcal{M}$y only sex partner has been Malcolm, and that was two years ago. I had never been with another man, ever. Hadn't even been on a date and now here I am standing in front of this Greek god-like man with no panties on, as he reached around me and unhooked my bra. He slid it to the floor slowly and I was standing here in all my glory while he was fully clothed. He rubbed his hand up and down my face before cupping my chin and lifting my face up to him. I wet my lips thinking that he was going to kiss me, but he didn't.

"Tell me what you want, Kriss," he told me.

What do you mean what I want, man? I'm standing here naked. I want to have sex, I thought.

"A kiss. I want you to kiss me," I whispered.

He leaned down and placed his lips on mine, and the chills that went down my body were... something. He pulled my bottom lip into his mouth and sucked on it softly. I didn't know what to do with my hands so I kept my hands clenched into fists at my side until he let my chin go, grabbed my hands, and wrapped them around his neck. He was kissing me so sensual and I noticed that I was losing my breath. He was sucking the breath out of me literally and blowing slightly back in my mouth. He pulled back momentarily, licked his lips, and smiled while I was trying to breathe.

"How... how were you doing that? You were taking my breath away with your kisses," I whispered.

"Don't worry about it. Just know that I'll always breathe for you."

"Unbutton my shirt, baby girl," he said.

I started unbuttoning his shirt and my eyes trailed up and down his body. My god he was built like a Greek god. I was secretly excited because I've heard that men that are built like him are not very huge in that department. That was the only thing that was stopping me from bolting out of the door. Once his shirt was off, I ran my hand up and down his chiseled abs and he chuckled.

"And you're forty," I said, still in disbelief.

"Yes, I am."

He laid me down on the bed and lay between my legs. His abs were laying right on my clit, applying pressure to it, making me want him even more. He started giving each of my protruding nipples a kiss before he took the right one between his lips while thumbing the other one. It felt so good to have a man touch me after two years that I didn't know what to do.

"Ahhh, it feels so good," I moaned out, and he responded by giving my left nipple the same amount of attention that he had given the right one.

By now, I was a leaking mess. I could feel my juices sliding down the crack of my ass and onto his comforter. He kissed down my stomach and took my bud between his lips and started to suck on her.

"That feels so good," I sighed as I stared at the moon that was shining through the glass.

Spence started dipping his tongue in and out of my hole and I scooted away from him because I couldn't take that pleasure anymore.

"Don't run from me, Kriss. You taste so damn good," he said and looked up at me.

He gripped my thighs and scooted me back down to him to continue his feast. He rubbed his hands up to my breast and gripped my neck... tight. The comforter was bunched up in my fist as I enjoyed the ride that Spence was taking me on. This man was a professional. He was not lapping at her like a dog licking water... these licks were very precise. He knew where and what he wanted to lick. I could feel the orgasm building as he continued to slowly lick up and down.

Pulling my bottom lip between my teeth, I let out a muffled groan. If I screamed as loud as I wanted to, I would definitely crack these windows. I tried to move, but I was stuck under his tight grip around my neck.

"Mmmmhhh," I groaned.

"Mmm-huh," he groaned while he continued to lick on her.

"Travisssss," I yelled his name as my juices came pouring out of me.

My body was shaking so fast as I was coming into his mouth. He drank every bit of me and my body fell flat to the bed. It was like I could see my soul levitating out of my body and descending past his glass roof. I hadn't felt this good in so long. I was so satisfied with that orgasm that I just wanted to go to sleep. I didn't even need to get any of his pipe. Come to think of it, I'm sure with head that fire, he was not packing in that area.

Through hooded eyes, I watched him stand up and jiggle his belt buckle. He slowly pulled his pants down and my mouth fell open at the print he was sporting through his briefs. I sat up and touched them because they were shiny. They felt really good.

"Is that—"

"Pure silk. Derek-Rose brand. I can get you some if you want. They feel really good and are very comfortable."

I shook my head because I didn't want him buying me anything. He slid his briefs down and... *it* popped up. Not out... up... past his belly button. The length and width of that thing is scary. He had a long and thick vein protruding up the bottom of it. He gripped it and started stroking it. The mushroom shaped head started to ooze, which lets me know that he was ready to enter me.

"Lay back, mama."

"I'm scared, Travis. It's been two years. I don't think... I can't... I won't be able to take that. You're going—"

"To take my sweet time inside of you and give you something that you've never had," he whispered and slowly laid me back. "Make you feel something that you never felt before," he spoke and hooked my legs in arms, snatching me closer to him. "And give you the biggest and best orgasm you ever had in your life," he whispered in my ear and pushed the head inside of me, prompting my mouth to open, but nothing fell out.

"Relax, Kriss, and let me in here," he said and kissed my cheek.

I closed my eyes as he thrust more inside of me, making me latch on to his humongous arms.

"No, open your eyes and look at me, Kriss," he ordered me.

I opened my eyes and stared into his eyes as he pushed more inside of me. My walls relaxed for him but not enough for him to put the whole thing in me.

"That's enough, Travis. Oh my God!" I moaned.

He was biting the corner of his bottom lip as he stroked half of his shaft in and out of me. I wrapped my legs around him, enjoying every moment of it. The pleasure wave is what Travis had me riding on. He was so careful with my body. Since my legs were wrapped around him, he leaned forward to get a good angle and he pushed it all the way inside of me, making me yelp out in pain.

"That... that was all of it," I whispered as he started to stroke me slowly.

He pulled out and I could hear her pop because she was so tight around him. He thrusted himself back inside of me.

"That was all of it, baby. You needed all of it," he said and kissed my cheek before pushing his tongue in my mouth, making me taste myself.

"Kriss, you feel amazing. You taste amazing. Everything about you is amazing," he groaned as he started to pummel me.

"Travissss," I moaned.

"Yeah, baby. You like this?"

Unable to speak, I nodded my head up and down quickly.

"Tell me, baby. Tell me you like this. Tell me you want more. Tell... me."

"There...is... more?" I queried.

He couldn't possibly be able to give more pleasure than he is giving me right now.

"Yes, baby girl. There is more."

He pulled out of me and flipped me over in one motion. He pulled my bottom half up in the air, forcing my body into a perfect arch for him. He spread my cheeks and ran his tongue up and down my crack one time before I fell flat to the bed. I had never had that before and it felt so damn good.

"Oh my god! I can't believe—"

"I'm a grown ass man, Kriss. Ain't nothing off limits. Toot that ass back up here," he growled.

I poked my butt back up at him and he assaulted my ass. He pushed his tongue in my ass hole while pushing two fingers inside of my love box, and used his other hand to thumb my swollen bud. My body started to convulse, which meant I was about to have a huge orgasm.

My cries of pleasure were muffled because my face was flat into the comforter. After I finished coming, I thought that Spence would be done, but he wasn't. He got on his knees and pushed himself back inside of me, making me squeal. He pushed my back down, making my arch even more perfect. He leaned over and started biting my shoulder.

"Look at me, baby," he whispered.

I turned my head towards him and he started kissing me while he stroked me slowly... precise strokes, just as he was licking on my pearl. This man knew how to pleasure a woman.

"Kriss, since I ran into you, I've wanted to know what you smelt like. What you taste like. What your hair smelled like. Everything. I wanted to have you screaming my name... turn you into my lil' woman. Damn. You feel so good. You smell so good. I pray to the man above that this is not my first and last time getting this. I'm begging you."

How could I respond to that with my walls being stretched as wide as they were? He wrapped his hands up in my hair and started to pummel me. His moans and groans turned into grunts. Letting me know that he was about to finish. The way he sounded had my body working overtime. I knew that I was getting ready to come right along with him.

"Uuggghhh," I groaned. "I'm about to comeee Travis."

"Me too, baby girl. Can I come in you? I don't want to pull out," he cried out.

"Come in me, Travis. Come... in... me..." I groaned as I started pushing back on him, matching his strokes.

"Oooowwee, baby girl. Throw it back on me then. Throw it back on me..."

I closed my eyes as the wave of pleasure came over me, making water pool in my eyes. I had never had an orgasm so intense that it made me cry before. He grunted one more time and I felt him erupt inside of me. He had come and come hard. He lay inside of me until he had grown soft. He pulled out and fell next to me on the bed. We were both trying to catch our breath. My body was spent, but he didn't lie.

He had given me the best sex that I had ever had.

"That was the best I ever had, baby girl," he commended.

"Likewise. I'm going to use the bathroom," I said.

I slid off the bed, grabbed my phone out of my bag, and hobbled into the bathroom. My middle was throbbing from the beating that Spence had put on it. I looked at my missed calls and saw that Lawrynn and Russ had both called me numerous of times. I called her back when I sat on the toilet. As soon as I pushed a little, the remnants of Travis came spilling out of me.

"GIRL! I HAVE BEEN CALLING YOU AND CALLING YOU! WHERE ARE YOU? WHERE WERE YOU?"

"Um," I whispered. I don't know why the hell I'm whispering because my whole room could fit in this bathroom twice. "I'm at Spence's house," I sniffed.

"You crying? What did he do? Where does he live?"

"In a huge ass house. I'm crying because he just gave me four of the best orgasms in my life, Lawrynn. I had never had anything like this before. I have never cried during an orgasm. Oh my god! He couldn't even fit in me at first."

"How did you expect him to beat it up? He a vet in the game girl. I'm so proud of you," she laughed.

"This will never happen again. Walking around this house made me feel a way. I can't offer this man nothing but my snatch. He has a hundred million dollars' worth of cars, Lawrynn. LAW... his freaking closet is two stories. He has stairs in his closet. Who do you know that has a two-story closet? I'm nowhere near his tax bracket. I can't... I can't stay here with him," I said.

"Girllll, don't ever down yourself to me or him, ever. You'll be the best wife that anyone would be lucky to have. Stay with him, and get another round in for me and then take your ass home in the morning and reminisce about it. Love you, bye," she said and hung up the phone.

I finished using the bathroom, washed my hands, and walked back out to the room. The moonlight was shining bright into the room. He had his back to me and I could see the tattoos etched into his toned back. I slid in the bed and started to trace them with my finger. He scared me when he grabbed my wrist and wrapped it around his body. He kissed each of my fingers before placing it on his chest and falling back asleep. I laid against his warm back, but I couldn't fall asleep.

An hour after laying awake, I decided that I couldn't stay here. He got what he wanted and I got what I wanted. I had fun, but this was the end of the road for us.

Spence

*M*y eyes flickered open and a smile immediately etched across my face. Kriss really got the best sex I had ever had in my life. She was so warm and tight. She felt as if she had never been touched before in life. If she had of never told me she had sex before, I would have thought that she was a virgin. She took my man good once she finally relaxed for me. I turned over and she was gone. The bathroom door was closed, so I thought that she was in there, but when I looked across the room and saw that her bag was gone, I jumped up out of the bed. I checked my pockets and her ID was gone. I sat down and put my head in my hands. I looked at the night stand and a piece of paper with writing was on there. I picked it up and started reading.

Travis, I had such a great time last night. Thank you for treating my body the way that it needed to be treated. This may be a stretch and you may not even want a relationship with me, but if you were thinking about it, let me just stop you and tell you that we are not compatible. I'm a coward and couldn't look you in your eyes and tell you that. Sorry.

I balled the paper up and threw it across the room. Who is she to tell me that she is not compatible to me? What does that even mean? I picked my phone up and went into my contacts, but her name was gone. I went into my call log and it was gone. It's crazy that she would do that when I know where she works at and where she lives. I was pissed at myself for leaving her file at work so I could get her phone number, and I didn't feel like going to my office on Sunday. My phone vibrated in my hand and it was my mom.

"Hello," I answered.

"I've been calling you all morning. Are you joining us for Sunday brunch, son?"

"Yes, I am. I'm getting ready right now," I lied.

"Okay. See you there."

Every Sunday, my family meets at our cousin's restaurant for brunch. I wasn't particularly happy to go visit because last night, Kriss brought out feelings that I had suppressed for a long time. I had stopped thinking about being a chef until *she* brought it up. Ms. Non-compatible. Who does she think she is?

I got up and took care of my hygiene. I ain't feel like dressing up, so I opted for a pair of Levi's and a black Dolce and Gabbana t-shirt with my black Yeezy's. My mom is going to be livid when she sees me. She hates when I dress in jeans in public settings. If she had it her way, I would wear a suit everywhere. I made sure I had everything before I left the house.

When I pulled up to the restaurant, my brother was outside arguing with our sister. There ain't no telling what they were going back and forth about, and I don't even care. I got out and acknowledged them and they looked at me like I had two heads on my shoulders.

"Mom's gonna get you, Spence!" Trena said and walked inside.

"What's up, bro?" Trevor spoke and dapped me up. "You hit

that—"

"Careful," I warned my brother because he was getting ready to call Kriss out of her name.

"Careful? What does that mean? You got feelings for that bit— girl or something?" he questioned while eyeing me.

"Nah, nothing like that. She left me a note telling me that we weren't compatible."

"Left a note? And compatible? You're not compatible with her. Look where she works. She doesn't fit in with you Spence and you know it. Think about it as you... ummm... shall we say, dodging a bullet. Don't beat your—Ohhh, I get it. You in your feelings because you couldn't hurt her feelings first. Damnnnnnn, Spence. It's all good. She was just another piece of ass anyway..." he said while laughing, but I wasn't laughing with him. "Right, Spence? She was just another piece of ass... *right*, Spence?" he repeated while nodding his head and looking at me like I was crazy, wanting me to agree with him, but could I? Was Kriss just another piece of ass?

"Yeah, man. Let's go in here."

I had to change the subject because I ain't want him to know that I was truly feeling a way about her leaving like a thief in the night. I wondered if she was as innocent as she said she was. Maybe Nardo is pimping her out like he does the rest of the girls and he lied to me the first time he spoke to me about her. Maybe. Maybe she scanned my cards and is having a spending spree right now. I can't believe I had sex with her raw. What am I doing right now? Am I saying all these bad things because she left me, or am I salty because I'm feeling her and she had the nerve to tell me that I was not compatible with her.

"Hello, Travis the Third," my mom spoke to me, calling me by my whole name. "Why are you dressed that way?"

"He stressed out mama. His little rendezvous didn't go well last night with his little friend," Trevor joked.

My mom rolled her eyes to the ceiling. She hated that I was still doing my thing and not married, but the women that I did bring home, my mom hated them, so I don't understand her frustration.

"What's going on, son?" My dad stood and pulled me into an embrace.

"Same ole, same ole," I replied.

The waitress came and took our order and walked away. My family and I were having good conversation and were talking about everyone's upcoming week and how we were going to execute this week's goal of getting two major accounts, when I looked at the door and saw *her*. My heart stopped at the sight of her walking in with a guy and another girl. The guy had his arm around her and I recognized him as the guy in her booth the night I saved her from Aaron. So, he must have been her friend. I prayed that he was her friend because if he wasn't, I was going to show a different side of me. How dare she get out of bed with me to go be with him?

"Spence, I been talking to you for the last two minutes, what's got your attention?" Trena said and turned around and looked at Kriss and the people she was with.

"Ohh, snap! That's the little rendezvous I was telling y'all about," Trevor said, which prompted my parents to direct their attention to the trio.

"Wow, she's cute Spence... and young. What is she this time? Twenty-five, twenty-six—" Trena started.

"Mind your business, Trena," I said, never taking my eyes off her.

She had on a nude strapless dress that stopped right below her knees paired with a pair of six inch heels that I would love to bend her over in. The dress was hugging everything that she had to give. The dress was v-cut, so her cleavage was pouring out of the dress. Her flat stomach looked very toned in that dress. I could tell from here that she didn't have on any panties, and just the thought of her standing in front of me with no panties on last night, had my blood flowing to my lower region. Her hair was pulled into a huge ball on top of her head and she wore large, gold hoop earrings in her ear with a diamond blinging in the second hole. Her skin was glowing, and I know that it was because of me.

She was rearing her head back and laughing at something the young man was whispering in her ear, and I hated that I felt jealous. She never even looked this way. How can she not feel me looking at her? I know the way we bore into each other's eyes last night, we connected on a different level. She can't tell me that she didn't feel what I felt last night. Compatible? What? I don't even understand. The more she laughed at that dude probably telling corny ass jokes, the more my blood started to boil. At this point, I could hold my hand out and you could boil an egg on it.

"Spence," Trevor nudged me in my side and then leaned over and whispered in my ear. "You got it bad for that girl? Because your jaw muscles are doing that thing it does when you get mad."

"I'm good, bro," I said to him, as the waitress sat our food and drinks in front of us. Before the waitress could set everybody's food down, I had downed my mimosa. I told her to bring me two more and my mom squinted her eyes at me.

"Travis the Third, are you okay?" my mom asked me.

I nodded my head in response to her. I swear I've only known this girl for two whole days and now I feel like I'm losing my mind because she is sitting in here with another man.

By the time they were seated, her back was to me. They sat at a four-seated table, so they had to be waiting on a fourth person. If it's a dude, then I'll know for sure that they are on a brunch date and I'll have every right to show my ass. Right?

After my family stopped focusing on me, they started talking about something else, but I felt like I was on autopilot. I was hearing them, but I wasn't responding. I was doing okay until I saw another dude walk in, hug Kriss, squeeze her ass, and then sit down. I downed the last of my third mimosa and scooted back from the table and got up.

"Look at him go," my brother said and snickered like a kid.

I walked over to the table and grabbed her arm, making her turn around.

"Is this what you meant when you said that we weren't compatible?" I questioned her.

"Spence—" she called my name in the sweetest voice.

"You let this guy touch and grab all on your ass, but I'm not compatible with you?"

"Travis—"

"WHAT!" I shouted at her.

"Aye, my man, you need to chill out," Mr. Ass Grabber stood and tried to defuse the situation.

"Let me talk to you outside, Kriss," I said to her, trying to keep my cool.

"Oh, now you wanna talk to me outside? You just came over here and embarrassed both yourself and me, and *now* you wanna talk outside. ARE YOU KIDDING ME?" she stood up and yelled in my face.

I stepped closed to her and whispered in her ear, "You either step outside voluntarily or I'mma throw you over my shoulder involuntarily in front of this crowded restaurant."

"You wouldn't," she growled in my ear.

I looked at her with a surprised look on my face and bent my knees a little to grip her thighs to hoist her over my shoulder. Yes, I carried her out of the restaurant kicking, screaming, and banging her fist into my back. Her little fist wasn't doing anything to me. It was quite therapeutic. I can see the headlines tomorrow, *Billionaire Travis Spencer drags screaming vixen out of restaurant.*

When we made it outside and out of the restaurant and around the building, I sat her down on her feet. She sighed hard before turning around and walking away with her hands on her head. She turned back around and glared at me. Those eyes turned into slits, and her cheeks would be red if she had been a lighter color.

"You are freaking unbelievable Travis! You don't know me and you embarrass me up in there in front of people. How dare you pick me up like that?" she snapped at me while rolling her neck, looking sexy as hell.

"How dare you leave me in the middle of the night, talking about we not compatible. What does that mean?" I asked her, and she tried to dart around me, but I moved in front of her.

"Nah, you ain't about to get around me until you explain to me what that means."

"Travis, you are a billionaire! A freaking billionaire! What can a girl who only gets by on tips do for you!?" I shouted at him.

"Nothing. There is nothing... *absolutely* nothing you can do with my son," I heard my mom's voice say behind me.

She chuckled lightly before replying, "Exactly."

She brushed by me and walked away. I looked past my mom's disgusted look on her face and watched that ass jiggle while she walked away. I was going to get her and she was going to be mine, and I'll do whatever I have to do.

Kriss

I was so annoyed by Travis's intrusion that I didn't even want to eat anymore. My friends and I were wanting to try this brunch spot. I never thought that I would run into Spence and he would react that way. I was low-key turned on, but I wouldn't let him know that. I walked back in the restaurant and marched to the table that I shared with Lawrynn, Russ, and her little brother. He always grabbed my ass when he hugged me. That's it.

"GIRL! What the hell was that?" Lawrynn asked.

"Neither one of you got up to see what was going on. He could have taken me around there and killed me," I hissed.

"Pssshhh. Taken you around there and gave you that—"

"LAW!" I shouted at her. "I lost my appetite. So, I'm just going to go home and sulk. We can try this again next Sunday."

I grabbed my purse and stomped out the door. I could see out my peripherals that Travis was still arguing with his mother. Just from that one sentence today, I knew that nothing else could happen between us because for the simple fact that she already don't like me and she doesn't even know my name.

I backed out of my parking space just as him and his mom was walking back into the restaurant. How can a man I have only known for such a short period of time have me so flustered? I mean, when I snuck out of his house in the wee hours of the morning, and caught an Uber to my car, he was the only thing that was on my mind. When I woke up this morning, he was the only thing on my mind. It must be the sex. That's what I'm going to go with because there is no way that he should be on my mind this heavy. God the sex was so good. I'm sure he gives that thing to every girl who comes his way. I wondered if he could even be monogamous. He probably wants to have two or three wives along with two mistresses. God, I gotta stop thinking about him.

I pulled in my driveway and my dad was just getting out of his car. He had just come from church. He looked nice in his three piece suit. I followed him inside of the house and into the kitchen. He had made a casserole last night and all he had to do was put it in the oven. We were going to have casserole and cornbread.

"Hey, night owl. You worked extra late last night?"

"No," I whispered and looked at the floor.

"What's wrong, Pumpkin?"

"I did a bad thing, Dad. Your boss...I had... last night and then... I don't know," I shrugged.

"You just said a whole bunch of nothing, little girl. You know you can tell me anything," he said and placed the casserole in the oven.

"I had sex with your boss last night but I left his house and left a note telling him that we are not compatible but now I think I like him... a little," I said quickly.

"He's forty, Kriss."

"I know."

"You're twenty-seven, Kriss."

"Again, I know. I told him that we weren't compatible, but not because of our age differences, Dad. It's because he's a billionaire and well... I'm a broke-naire. I don't have anything to offer him. I still have bills that I am trying to pay down. I don't want him to think that I am using him for money. You know?"

"He's forty," my dad said again. "Why do you keep talking about what you have to offer him or whatever? I won't approve of that, Kriss Brown! You're like a disposable razor to him. Do you know how many women he has had coming in and out of his office every other day having sex with them? I know for a fact last month four ladies came within one week to see him. I don't want him to hurt you and that is exactly what he is going to do."

"Dad," I whispered.

"NO! I don't want to hear anything else about it," he said and waved me off.

I went upstairs and dived in the bed. This is one of the worst fights that me and my dad have had in forever. Every big fight that we have had was about a boy. He hated Malcolm and I think that is also one of the reasons that I stayed with him for as long as I did because I wanted to prove him wrong, but he ended up being right.

Later that night...

It was storming like crazy in Atlanta and the only thing I could think about was the fact that Travis has a glass roof and he is getting a good view of the lightning storm that is happening outside. I am so happy that I don't work on Sundays. It was one in the morning and I turned over in the bed wondering if Travis was thinking about me... even after I yelled at him at the restaurant earlier today. I got up and put on some clothes because I was going to go over there. I wanted to sleep in his arms and I didn't care what my dad said. I was going to do a pop up visit. I'll look like a fool if he has another girl over there, but it is worth a try. I felt like a teenager sneaking out of my dad's house when I closed the door as quietly as I did, even though I was a grown woman.

It took a while to find his house but when I did, I pulled up to his gate, let my window down, and pressed the speaker button. Moments later his voice came through the speaker.

"Only compatible people are allowed in here."

"Don't be a baby, Travis. Open the gate."

"I said only compatible—"

"One date, Travis. One date!" I cut him off.

I heard a beep and the gate opened. I drove my car up the driveway and parked behind a white Audi. I got out the car and ran up to the door because my umbrella was raggedy. The door opened as soon as I got to the top step. When I stepped into the house, I started shivering because I was cold.

"Stay here, let me get you something to put on," he ordered.

He was back in a flash with a teal blue shirt and a towel. I got undressed right at the door and he dried me off, and I put on the shirt and it felt and smelled so good. The shirt stopped right under my butt cheeks.

"What kind of shirt is this? Is this like your briefs you had on?"

"Yes. I told you I can get you a set of pajamas from Derek-Rose if you would like," he said and led me to his kitchen.

"I'll fix you some tea with lemon, so you won't get sick. Wait... why are you here? You don't work on Sundays so..."

"How do you know that?"

"Um, I know everything."

"Right. I should have known. With money, you can find out anything."

"That's true, but answer the question."

"I wanted to know what it was like to look at the ceiling while the rain was pouring down on it," I replied. "And I was thinking about you," I admitted a little lower.

"What was that last part, baby girl?" he asked with a smirk on his face.

I rolled my eyes at him. The kitchen was silent until the teapot went off. He poured me some tea in a tea cup and I stared at the steam that was coming off the tea.

"What were you thinking about?"

"How after two days, I like you... a little. How I want to date you, but I'm scared and I can't. My dad doesn't approve of you because you're—"

"Forty," we both said at the same time.

"And plus, my dad said that you have a lot of girls coming and going out of your office. Is that true?"

"It is."

"Is that why you're not married? You haven't found a girl to be in a polygamous relationship with you?"

"No, I just don't want to get married or I haven't met a woman worth marrying... yet."

He eyed me after that last comment. When he said that I got quiet and took a sip of my tea. I wondered what that comment meant. This has to be some type of phase that I am going through or something because I am really feeling him. God, please take it away.

"Can we talk more about the compatible comment, Kriss?"

Sighing, I said, "Travis, like I told you earlier, you are a billionaire—"

"SO!"

"—and I make money from tips."

"SO!"

"I have had two degrees for two years and I can't work in my field because of my student loans and my credit. I don't want people to think that I'm using you for your money. I don't want to be your trophy wife; I want to work. I love numbers. I am really good with numbers. Your mom doesn't like me already and I don't want to deal with people who don't like me. They can become unbearable. I fall in love fast and that can be my downfall. You're forty and I'm twenty-seven. You have lived a lot and I have a lot of life to live. I want kids one day and you don't want kids at all. It's just so much that I feel like we are not compatible on. Sex is magical and something I never had before, but I think that is as far as we can go," I vented to him.

"Thank you for explaining that to me, Kriss. I'll be back in a moment," he said and left me sitting at the kitchen table.

Moments later he came back with his computer. He pulled me up from my seat and pulled me down on his lap. He opened his laptop and went to Nelnet, the student loan website.

"Let me see how much you owe, maybe I can help you out," he said.

"See, that is not what I want you to do, Travis," I whined.

"Open...up...your...account, Kriss."

I sighed and typed in my information. I instantly covered up the screen because that number always broke my damn heart because it's going to take me forever to pay off a two hundred-thousand-dollar student loan. Shit, education should be free. I don't know what the United States is waiting on.

He moved my hand out of the way and didn't even flinch when he saw where the comma and period was placed. He clicked on 'Pay full amount' and his credit card information came up.

"No. No, no—"

"Too late," he said and chuckled after pressing complete payment.

The screen came back on and the balance was zero. My heart

started beating so hard and fast because I couldn't believe that in one stroke of a keyboard, my student loans were gone. Wow.

"Go to your other credit cards."

"Travis, I can't ask you..."

"What did I say? Don't question when someone is trying to help you."

For the next thirty minutes, I watched as he sat and clicked 'pay full amount' on every credit card I own. I watched him click 'pay full amount' on all my collections. I was frozen because I couldn't believe that he had done that for me.

"Thank you so much, Travis," I said and kissed him on the cheek.

"Let's go to bed, mama."

I got up and followed him to the bedroom. I couldn't wait to cuddle up under him and properly thank him for doing that for me. I went from drowning in debt to debt free in thirty minutes. My life really could be looking up.

Spence

I was happy that I could do that for Kriss because she deserved it. Nobody that has two degrees should be working at a bar unless they really want to. I led her to the bedroom and we slid onto my silk sheets. We both were staring at the rain falling against the glass, and I was rubbing my fingers through her hair.

"So, your mom doesn't like me, huh?"

"No, but she doesn't like anybody. So, don't consider yourself special."

I know she saw my mom and I having a disagreement, and we were having a disagreement about her. I told her that Kriss was twenty-seven and she lost it before I could even tell her about her two degrees from Spelman, which is the school that she graduated from. I came home and started preparing for my work week. Trust me, Kriss showing up to my house was a very pleasant surprise, but I wasn't mad at all. I could use her company.

"So, are you going to stay with me tonight or do I have to wake up with you gone again?"

"I'm going to stay, Travis, I promise. Also, I'm surprised that you don't have a team of people running up and through here all day every day."

"I do. They just don't work on the weekends. My assistant is Zahara, and my stylist is Jaquel. They are sisters. I'm sure you'll meet them. I have a cook, a maid, and a butler. It's just me and I don't have a lot of company, so they really just be here chilling."

"So, about our one date? When is it going to be?"

"Our one date is going to be tomorrow night. I already set the reservations earlier today."

"Huh? How did you do that? You ain't know I was going on a date with you."

"Yes, I did. I'm part psychic on most days."

She started cracking up and I knew then that I was going to like her more than I wanted to because of the way she laughed at my corny joke. Her laugh was so cute.

"You keep playing in my hair, I'm going to go to sleep, Mr. Spencer."

"Ugh! That just made me go flaccid. Mr. Spencer is my dad."

There was that laugh again. I pulled her on top of me and stared up at her. She leaned down and started kissing on me. She pushed her tongue in my mouth and I happily accepted it. I started kissing her like it would be my last time kissing her. I started sucking on her tongue and I could feel her getting wet on my abdomen. Listen, this woman leaks like a broken faucet. God knew what He was doing when He created her. My God!

She pulled away from the kiss and started kissing on my neck. Placing soft kisses up and down my neck had me rock hard, and he was curving up trying to escape my briefs. When she took my earlobe in her mouth, I could feel myself starting to ooze. When she started placing kisses behind my ear, my mans started to hurt because of the way he was straining against my briefs.

"That's my spot baby," I whispered.

She reached behind her and unbuttoned the one button that was holding my man hostage, and she freed him. She started stroking him while still kissing behind my ear. She lifted herself up and eased down on him slowly, making me inhale very sharply. God, I had never felt anything like this before in my life. This girl was so tight around me and she knew it. If she squeezes her muscles around me one good time, she'll make me come so fast.

"You like that?" she whispered in my ear.

"Yes, baby, I love it. That's the perfect speed... right there. Keep going..." I groaned.

She sat up and I had a full view of her sliding up and down. Her cream was so thick and white and I wanted to close my eyes, but I didn't want to miss anything. She started to speed up but I had to grab her waist to slow her down because I did not want to come.

"Good Lord, Kriss, why do you feel this good, girl?" I groaned.

She turned around and with my man still inside of her, she leaned over and took off on my man like it would be the last time she rode anything.

"Ahhh, Kr-Kr-Kr... Ahhh," I groaned.

Goddddd, she had me stuttering. I could feel my come building up in my scrotum. I started thrusting myself up inside of her hard.

"You couldn't even take me last night, now you are taking over. I like that, baby girl."

I could feel her muscles clenching me which made me erupt... hard inside of her and she kept going. Even after she came, she kept going. My head was so sensitive and the more it pressed against her g-spot, the more I could see my soul levitate from my body. She had, as the young people say, 'snatched my soul.' She turned around again and lay on my chest with me still inside of her. I wrapped my arms around her as she snuggled up in the crook of my neck. I know for a fact that I'm going to be tired as hell in a few hours at work.

€€€€€

"Spence!" Zahara shouted my name.

Slightly jumping when my name was called, I immediately responded, "Yes, Zahara," as if I had been paying attention the whole time.

"Damn, nice of you to finally join us in this meeting. You've been sitting there staring idly at that wall for the last twenty minutes. You okay?" Trevor asked me with a crazy look on his face.

"Yeah, I'm good," I replied, but I wasn't.

We were having our weekly Monday team meeting. I was sitting at the head of the table and looking out at my team. Trevor always led these meetings and I would add my input in every now and then. I was sitting here physically, but mentally I was somewhere else. That somewhere else being in between Kriss's legs. Thirty minutes before my alarm went off, I was awakened to some of the best head I ever had in my life. Her mouth was warm and wet and she had me screaming like a woman in my own damn house. All I could do was look down at her as she continued to suck on him. I hadn't had him sucked that good since that crazy broad I had to fire. I wondered if Kriss was crazy. I really hope not. The minute my alarm went off, this girl begged me to give her some wood and of course, I obliged. I had the most beautiful black woman in the world in my bed begging for sex; of course I was going to give it to her.

She was the reason that I was also thirty minutes late for work. After I finally got dressed, she gave me a kiss goodbye. A long kiss goodbye. I told her that she could stay in my home and enjoy a hearty breakfast by my chef, and she said that she would. She looked so damn good in my pajama shirt that I really wanted to bend her over and give her a few strokes for the road.

"I think we will have that new condo account by Wednesday," one of my senior architects spoke.

"Good," I responded.

I was finally starting to shift my focus when the door burst open and in walked Kriss being dragged by the wrist by her father. She looked embarrassed, and her eyes were puffy as if she had been crying. She still had on my pajama shirt which made me smile inside, but the scowl on her father's face let me know that this was not about to be a social visit. I braced myself for the embarrassment that would ensue.

"You stay the hell away from my daughter," he said, while pointing his finger in my face.

My brother stood, but I held my hand up to stop him. I stood and cleared my throat while pulling my blazer together before I started to speak, "Clear the room."

"No, they can stay. Stay the hell away from my daughter. She will not be your nut rag, Travis Spencer the Third. My daughter is twenty-seven years old and she cannot do anything for you. Stay away from her," he growled at me.

Mind you, Mr. Brown and I are the same height, so we were standing nose to nose while Kriss was behind him looking at the ground.

"What if I don't stay away from her? What are you going to do?" I questioned and cocked my head to the side.

"Dad, please," she whispered.

He turned to face her.

"NO, Kriss. I told you to stay away from him and the first thing your hot ass does is run over to his house in the middle of the night. This man does not care about you and he never will. You think he would give a damn about you? He's forty, unmarried, never been married, no kids and doesn't mess with women his own age. Let me remind you that you are just another notch in his belt... in his thousand dollar belt," her dad snapped at her.

She held her head down in shame, and I was now breathing fire out of my nose and trying to contain my anger in front of my team. Since we were in the first floor conference room, a crowd had gathered outside the door.

"Thirty-five hundred dollars. My belt was thirty-five hundred dollars," I corrected him, making him turn back and look at me.

I stepped closer to him and looked this man in his eyes to let this man know how I feel about him ambushing me and his daughter.

"Let me tell you something, Mr. Brown. Your daughter is so beautiful and I do like her...a lot. If she wants to come over my house in the wee hours of the morning, she is very welcomed to do so. I will date your daughter as long as she will allow me to. Your daughter is twenty-seven years old and can make decisions on her own. I won't apologize for my age and my status. So, if you don't mind, I think there is a bucket and a mop somewhere waiting on you. You're excused."

Before I could even comprehend what had happened, this man reared back and punched me in my nose. I wanted to attack him, but I had to remind myself that this was my elder and I know that I could kill him with two blows to the head. I could see him dragging Kriss away and she mouthed 'I'm sorry' before she was out of my sight.

My brother and Zahara handed me some napkins while I was walking out of the conference room. I rode the elevator up to my office while holding my bloody nose. Luckily, that man hadn't broken my nose.

Fifteen minutes later, my nose had stopped bleeding and I had changed my shirt. I wanted to text Kriss to apologize for what I said to her father. I know the mop and bucket comment was too far.

"Old man packs a punch, huh? I fired him, in case you're wondering," my brother said when he walked in my office.

"Why did you do that? I wasn't going to fire him. He has every right to feel that way. I am screwing his daughter and I'm not going to stop unless she wants me to."

"WHAT? He punched you in your nose in front of everyone. You know Mom and Dad are going to hear about that and are going to react terribly to this information. Wait, screwing? I thought it was only a one-time thing. What happened to being non-compatible?"

"She showed up to my house last night. I wasn't going to turn her away. For what? I like her and she likes me. He's going to lose his shit when he finds out that I been screwing her raw," I said and chuckled to myself.

"EXCUSE ME! You've been doing what?"

I looked up to see my mom was standing at the door along with my father.

"That's my cue," Trevor said while holding up his church finger.

"Boy, sit down," my dad ordered him, making me laugh a little.

"You don't know this girl from a can of paint and you are out here spilling your seeds inside of her. Apparently, you don't listen to anything me or your father says. That girl is no good for you, and you know it. She is the daughter of a cleaner for God's sake. What about the nice girl from church... Christian? She's a doctor and her dad is the senator."

"Ehhh, been there, done that, bought that t-shirt. Her box is not good and she's annoying," I admitted to my mom, making her and my dad's mouth fall open. "And Mom, if this is about age, isn't Dad ten years older than you?" I asked with my eyebrows furrowed together as if I didn't know the answer to that question already.

"This is not about your father and I," my mom huffed.

"Furthermore, wasn't grandfather a struggling journalist and grandmother was a librarian. Did they try and stop you from dating my father?"

"Spence, calm down. Maybe we need to revisit this conversation when tensions are not this high," my father spoke.

"No, we are going to have this conversation now, so we won't ever have to have it again. Are we clear? My love life is none of anyone's business... no more. I will date who I want to date... when I want to date them... and how I want to date them, regardless of their age, well if they are of age. Is that understood? We are not going to mention anything about *age* again. As far as anyone using anyone for money... so what? I won't spend a billion dollars in my lifetime and she can spend as much of my money as she wants. Also, Kriss doesn't care about money. *She* feels that I am out of her league, but I'm not. I like her... she likes me, and as long as she wants to date, we will. Now, if there isn't anything else..." I said, hoping that would end the conversation and they would leave.

"But son... you haven't even known her for a long time. Can you at least—" my mom started.

"No, I can't. Again, if there isn't anything else you would like to speak to me about..." I said and nodded my head towards the door.

My dad has always been kind of cool as far as my dating life; he just always wanted me to be careful and not get in any trouble fooling with these girls. My mom has always been critical, but that's the type of person that she is... extra.

My parents left out of my office and I had to listen to my brother rant and rave about me dating a bottle girl but what they don't know is, we haven't even started officially dating yet. The more people tried to pull us apart, the more I was going to want her. I can see it now.

Kriss

$\mathcal{I}$ hadn't spoken to my father in two weeks after he broke up Spence's meeting and sucker punched him in the nose, and I haven't spoken to Travis either because of that mop and bucket comment he made to my father. My father worked hard all his life and he loved cleaning, so for him to say that, pissed me off. I'd been to work, but I have been working the earlier shifts so I wouldn't run into him. Working the earlier shifts meant less tips, but I was fine with that, especially since all my credit card bills and stuff were paid off.

I hadn't even told my friends what happened, but I was going to go tell Law about it today. I'd been so depressed because the two days with Spence had me on cloud nine. Could you really like someone after two days? I feel like I don't know him at all to be lusting over him the way that I am. It had to be his charming ways that had me turned on to him. His smile was so bright. Or maybe it was his arms. Those guns are something out of a movie. You could tell that he worked out faithfully. Or maybe it was that magic stick. He knows exactly how to work it too. God, sex with him was so magical, and I wanted to do it repeatedly. I was addicted. After two days and multiple rounds, I was addicted.

"Hey, crackhead," Lawrynn called out getting my attention.

I put the magazine down that I was reading and walked into her office and sat down.

"Okay, why you been so distant over the last two weeks? I thought I was going to have to come peel you away from that rich man's arms, especially after he reacted in that restaurant, girllll! Listen! I know your box good because you had him going crazy after only one night," she said and laughed.

"Girl, that's not even the half of it. I told my dad about it and he FORBADE me from seeing him. That night I went to go see him and we had sex again. I feel like I'm addicted to him. He left me to go to work while I enjoyed breakfast with his chef. I went home in his pajama shirt and my dad was livid. I mean, it felt and even smelled expensive. I googled Derek-Rose pajamas and the shirt was five hundred dollars. ANYWAY... my dad dragged me like a bad child being dragged into the principal's office, into Spence's meeting."

"WHAT!"

"YES! Broke up Spence's meeting and didn't have a care in the world. They exchanged unpleasantries and then my dad sucker punched him in the nose. I could not believe that my dad had done that. So, I hadn't talked to neither one of them in two weeks."

"Wait, I missed what Spence did. Why did you stop talking to him?" she asked me.

"Well, amid the heated exchange, Spence told him 'there is a mop and a bucket waiting on you.'"

"Ouch!"

"Yes, girl! So, yeah, I was pissed about that. Anyways, I am debt free, now. He paid off allllll my student loans, collections, and credit cards. I begged him not to because you know how prideful I am, but he did it anyway."

"Girl, your head game must be immaculate."

"Shut-up."

"You wanna go grab lunch? I'm starving."

"Sure!"

We settled on the sandwich spot right around the corner from her office. We ordered and waited for our numbers to be called. I was sipping on my water and playing on my phone when this huge man approached me. I immediately recognized him as Spence's driver.

"Hello, Ms. Brown. I'm Rick—"

"I know who you are and I have no interest in talking to Travis Spencer the Third," I hissed.

"—and Spence requests your presence in the car. If you don't comply, I am instructed to pick you up, throw you over my shoulder, and carry you out of here. Ms. Brown, I don't want to do that." He completely ignored what I said.

Lawrynn was snickering at him, which pissed me off. I looked out the window and saw the big car holding up traffic. I waved him off and continued to sip on my water.

"Ms. Brown," he called my name.

"Get out of my face, Rick, and tell Spence to—ahhh," I squealed when Rick hoisted me over his shoulder as he promised he would.

As I was being carried out of the door, Lawrynn made the phone signal up to her ear and I rolled my eyes at her. She was being a horrible friend right now. Rick opened the back door of the truck and threw me in Spence's lap. Rick got in the truck and pulled off.

"You are unbelievable, Travis!" I growled at him.

He ignored me as he loosened the tie around his neck. I didn't know that a man loosening a tie could be so sexy.

"Rick," he called out, and the glass started sliding up.

"Come here," he ordered me.

"No."

"No?"

"You not used to hearing the word no, huh?"

"No, so come here," he said again.

"No."

He started chuckling and then unbuckled his belt. When he did that my heart started beating remarkably fast. I missed him... it... in fact, I craved him. There's a difference. Crave is a powerful desire for something. Yearn. I yearned for his touch. Him touching me is way different than when I touch myself. Over the last two weeks, I have been getting myself off and it just didn't feel right. I needed him to do it. I wanted him to do it.

Before I could react, he pounced on me...while Rick was in the front driving on a crowded street. The tint was super dark so no one would know what we were doing. That's what made it very sexy as well. I had on a pair of black Palazzo pants with a black off the shoulder crop top, so everything could come off easy. Before I could even blink, my pants were at my ankles and now on the floor. My top was pulled down and exposing my bare breast.

"You want this?" he growled.

"Want what?" I asked and licked my lips.

He took my hand and placed it on his shaft. He started growing into my hand and I started getting wetter than I already was. I was for sure about to mess up these leather seats.

"That? Do you want that?" he whispered, trying to contain his breathing.

His chest was rising and falling at a rapid pace. It looked as if he was struggling to breathe. Like... at any given moment he would combust if I didn't give him consent to touch me.

"I'm mad at you, Spence," I said.

"Please... Kriss," he whispered so low, it almost sounded like a whistle.

I grabbed his hand and brought it to my breast and let him grip it. He closed his eyes and started to caress it while biting that huge bottom lip. I looked at him stroking himself, and the semen that oozed from the head turned me on so much.

"Can I... I'm begging you. The last two weeks has not been the same without you...our connection... being in your presence, Kriss. I don't deserve..."

I grabbed his shaft and guided him to me... into me. He pushed past my folds slowly and carefully, like he didn't want to hurt me. We both let out groans of pleasure once my lips touched the base of his shaft. He hooked my legs in his arms and leaned over to place his lips on mine.

He started delivering long and slow strokes. Spence thrust all the way in and pulled all the way out until he heard my hole make that wet pop sound, like pulling a sucker out of your mouth. He continued to deliver those strokes while he leaned over and pushed his tongue in my mouth. I sucked on his thick tongue and tasted everything he had for lunch.

"Dammnn, baby girl," he moaned.

I couldn't even moan because my breath was caught in my throat.

He pulled back to look in my face and he asked, "How was your day, baby girl?"

Huh? How you expect me to answer that when you're digging in me like this? I shouted in my mind.

My mouth fell open, but I had no answer. I couldn't answer. My soul was leaving my body through my mouth when it opened. All I could do was try to suck it back in every time he pulled out of me, but it left again when he would push back in me. My GOD! This man! My breathing had changed because I was getting ready to burst. I was getting ready to rain down on him and he knew it because he sped the strokes up.

"Give it to me!" he groaned.

I didn't want to scream and scare Rick, so I sunk my teeth into Spence's neck and erupted hard on him. He didn't stop... in fact, he sped up even more. He started grunting and I wrapped my legs around him.

"Damn! Damn! Damn! Ahhh, Damn! Mmmhhh, Damn. You feel so good to me, Kriss," he groaned as he finished inside of me.

I couldn't even sit up because I was still feeling good from my orgasm.

"Come on, put your clothes on. Let's go inside and talk."

"Inside?" I queried.

I used my elbows to sit up and I saw that we were in front of his house. Right where I wanted to be.

Spence

She had been ignoring me for two weeks. Two whole weeks while I was over here sulking. I had gone up to her job and would sit there nightly waiting for her, but I never saw her. I had all types of thoughts running through my head. I thought that maybe she had quit because she didn't want to see me. I thought that maybe she had gotten everything she wanted out of me and I was truly a sucker, but then... Lawrynn. Her friend. She's a talker, but she told me that she had been dodging her as well, so she felt a way as well. I wasn't a sucker after all.

Now, we were in my kitchen and I was preparing a recipe for her that I saw on Pinterest. Yes, I look at meals on Pinterest.

"You need some help?" she asked when she walked into the kitchen.

I looked up at her and she was wearing another one of my pajama tops. We had a round of hot, steaming sex in the bedroom and then one in the shower, and her hair got wet. Her hair was up in a towel and she was glowing.

"No, I want you to just sit in here and keep me company. That's all," I replied to her.

She came and leaned against the counter and I placed a kiss on the tip of her nose.

"Kriss, I want to apologize to you for saying those awful things to your father. I know that's why you were ignoring me. I wasn't going to even fire him, but my brother did. I mean, if he wants to come back then he can. I don't have no problem with re-hiring him. I just..."

"He's not coming back. My dad is stubborn and I'm his only child, and he's really, really protective over me," she sighed.

"Does he need money?"

She shook her head and came and stood behind me, wrapping her arms around me and laying her head on my back.

"Spence, I want to date you... but I love my dad."

My heart started to race because I felt like she was trying to walk away from me again.

"I'll talk to him, Kriss."

"Didn't you just hear me say that my dad is stubborn?"

I turned around to face her.

"Don't you like me?"

"Yes, b—"

"No, buts."

She folded her lips in her mouth when I cut her off.

"I like you as well and I feel like we can actually build something together. You can't let your dad affect your happiness. Your happiness is much more important, and if I talk to your father, I will make him understand that. Well, not make him, but you know."

"What if he punches you again?"

"The first one, I understood because you are his baby... his only child, but if he tries to give me a right hook again, I'mma hit him with a left."

She smacked me in my chest and started laughing. She went and sat at the table and watched me prepare our meal for the night. I made lemon chicken with roasted vegetables. Something light.

"Spence, this tastes amazing," she said as she placed the second bite of chicken in her mouth. "It was a chef, huh? You wanted to be a chef? You never told me what you wanted to be instead of an architect, but if I had to guess, it was a chef."

I nodded my head.

"You should have told your dad that you weren't going to be an architect. Put your little Versace slipper down and told him that you weren't going to do it," she said and laughed.

"You're not funny you know that. I'm the first son... I'm supposed to, but it's all good, now. If you come here, I'll cook for you and that'll satisfy me. I just like to cook. My time to cook professionally is over.

"But it's not. Maybe you could host cooking classes or something once a month. You'll still get your fulfillment. That's a hot thing, ya know. You can teach couples how to cook some aphrodisiacs or something like that."

"But I'm not a chef. My cousin is one though."

"Great! Have your cousin come and assist you, so you can say a licensed chef will be present."

"Hmph, I never thought of that. How you know people will

come?"

"TUH! Do you not know who you are?" she said and reached in her bag and pulled out a magazine and flipped through it and slammed the magazine down in front of me. "You are Travis Spencer the Third, the hot, single billionaire. Trust me. The birds will be clucking," she said, making me double over from laughter. "Atlanta's Most Eligible Bachelor my ass. I'mma cut somebody if you pipe another girl down the way you just did me."

"You're the only one I want," I said to her, and I couldn't believe that I was serious.

We finished dinner and had a very nice conversation. Although I already knew everything about her from her file, it was good to hear it from her. I told her about my families. She looked at her watch and said that it was time for her to take a nap, so she could get to work. I wanted to protest but I didn't, but once she becomes my girl, she will not be working for that scumbag, Nardo. He already been texting me and asking me what was going on between us, but I had been ignoring him.

€€€€€

After dropping Kriss off to her car, I followed her to make sure she got to work fine. I sat in the parking lot thinking.

"Rick, you think I should go over and talk to Mr. Brown? You're older. You have a daughter around Kriss's age. Would you be mad if I wanted to date her?"

He eyed me through the rearview mirror.

"Knowing you personally, yes. You know you run through women like crazy, but I see the way you are with Ms. Brown. You really like her. I've been working with you for a long time and I've never seen you act this way. Also, you've had sex with her more times than you can count. What woman can say that?"

"You're right," I said. "I still think that I should talk to him, man to man. I want us to have some type of understanding, ya know."

"You've always been an upfront guy, so I don't expect anything less from you."

I gave him the address to Kriss's home and we were there in the next forty-five minutes. I thought about everything I would say to him. I mean, I know he's going to be mad that I'm showing up on his doorstep at midnight, but I wanted to get this off my chest because I wanted Kriss with me and in my bed when she gets off from work.

Rick opened the door for me and followed me up to the door step. I rang the doorbell and waited for few minutes. He opened the door and I was staring down the barrel of a shotgun. Rick reached for his gun, but I held my hand up to stop him.

"I come in peace," I said with my hands up.

"What are you doing here? Where is my daughter? I know she's with you," he said and cocked the shotgun.

"Spence!" Rick called my name.

"Everything is fine, Rick," I assured him. "Mr. Brown, Kriss is at work. I came to talk to you man to man," I said to him.

"Man to man? Man to man about what? You don't want nothing with me."

"Yes, I do. I came here to discuss Kriss. Let me in, sir. It'll be quick, I promise."

"NO! I'm not letting you in here. I know your type. You're filthy rich. You just want to get with my daughter to brainwash her into thinking that I never loved her because I didn't give her the life that you can give her. You trying to take my only baby away from me. Get her across town in that big house and flash money and diamonds in her face, and I'll never see her again," he vented.

"Mr. Brown, take the gun away from my face, so we can talk, ok? I want to step inside and talk to you about your concerns. Please," I begged.

After a couple minutes of silence between us, he slowly lowered the gun and moved so Rick and I could come in.

"You make one wrong move and I'll be using my *mop and bucket* to clean up the blood," he said.

He led us to the kitchen and we took a seat while Rick stood behind me. He looked up at Rick and then back at me.

"Do he got to look serious all the time?"

"Well, when a man is holding a shotgun on the man that he is supposed to protect, I think that can cause a man to look serious," I said and chuckled, trying to lighten the mood.

"Okay, so talk."

"Mr. Brown, first let me apologize for the very insensitive comment that I made regarding you being a janitor. Your job is as important as mine and I'm truly sorry for saying that. I'll never say

116

anything like that again and I wasn't going to fire you; that was my brother's doing. I can give you a severance package or hire you back if..."

"I'll take both," he said and laughed.

"Done. Fifteen thousand and you can come back to work whenever you want to."

"Stop trying to butter me up. I'm still skeptical of you trying to date my twenty-seven-year-old daughter."

"About that, Mr. Brown. Kriss is so funny and so smart and I just want to date her. I'm not trying to marry her...yet. She's so beautiful and her heart is so good. I'm not trying and nor will I ever try to take her away from you. I'm very family oriented myself, so there is no way that she would go days without seeing you. I know you are skeptical because of my age, my status, all of that, and you have every right to be because I would be too if some old rich man was trying to date my daughter but honestly, Kriss doesn't care about my money; she just wants to have fun and..."

"Careful."

"You're right, but you get what I'm saying."

"I'm trying to but Kriss is my only daughter. I had to console her during her first bad breakup. She was depressed for weeks behind that no good scoundrel. The nerve of him to be laid up on my baby girl's birthday. She hasn't celebrated a birthday ever since she caught him with a girl on her birthday. On her birthday. Then he tried to tell her that he was in a car accident, not knowing that she had already seen him naked with the woman."

"Wow," I sighed.

I guess that's why she hated Malcolm and never wanted to talk about him.

"Listen, Spence... I love my baby so much. She is the only person I have since I lost my wife when she was born. I don't ever want her to suffer a heartbreak anymore. She doesn't deserve that and if you can't give her the happiness that she deserves, then I don't want you to even date her."

"Mr. Brown, I won't promise you that I will never hurt her, because I will, but it won't be intentionally. Everything is not going to be peaches and cream between us. There are some days I may have to cancel a date because of an urgent meeting I have to take. There are some days where I may work eighteen hours a day and don't come to bed until she's asleep."

"Why you talking about beds and stuff if all you want to do is date her?" he asked. "Y'all dating in the bed?"

You don't know the half.

"You don't want me to answer that, Mr. Brown."

"I sure in the hell don't. I don't even know why I asked."

"Listen, the bottom line is, I can see us moving past dating. I want to make sure everything is okay between us before I pursue her... hard. Make sure she knows that she is the only one I will be dating."

He squinted at me and continued to stare at me for what felt like three hours but was really thirty seconds.

"Alright, you have my blessings, but if you hurt my daughter one time with any of your shenanigans, this thing will put to bed."

We stood and shook hands and I left his house feeling I had accomplished something.

Kriss

My heart was beaming through the roof because of the email that I just got. I had just landed a job as a Junior Accountant starting with a salary of seventy thousand dollars. I couldn't wait to get home to tell Spence about my job. I was at the mall with Lawrynn and Russ having lunch. We have been officially dating for two months and I was loving it. Well, being alone with him because when I was out in public, cameras were in my face asking me questions about being with the billionaire, and it was the most annoying thing ever, but because it was Spence it was worthwhile. I could not believe that he had stepped to my dad like that and told him that. My dad had gone back to work at Ground-Up and he was happier than ever. He even quit his second job because of the healthy raise that Spence had given him.

"I got the job, people!" I squealed.

"Of course you did because you are great and smart as hell," Russ said.

"That's great. Now you can go and officially quit your job at 227," Lawrynn said.

For the last two months, I had gone from working six nights to four to one night a week. Nardo was pissed because again, I was his best girl and men would come and ask for me and I would be gone and they would leave. I wonder if Spence would have a problem with me continuing to work one night a week. He probably would because I worked nights, and he would be acting like a baby when I come home from work and he's in the bed staring at the ceiling. Home. Yes, I moved in with him and I don't care that we haven't even made anything official. When you know... you know. My dad was skeptical and thought that we were moving too fast, but I was happy, and if it didn't work out then it just didn't work out, and I could always move back into the house with my dad.

Before I could reply to her, I heard my name being called from behind me. I turned around to see that Malcolm was calling me while he was holding the hands of two kids. If I wasn't happy with Spence I would be feeling a way.

"Hey, how are you?" he asked, walking up to the table.

"She good, my man. Don't worry about how she is doing." I turned to see Spence walking up.

Spence was much taller and broader than Malcolm and I knew that he didn't want any problems with him. I stood and kissed him sloppily and Malcolm smacked his lips and walked away.

"What are you doing here, baby?" I asked him.

"Nothing, I was coming to see you since I was about to grab lunch for the team across the street at Crab Shack. We got the account for the new development that will be opening next year."

"Congrats baby!" I hugged him. "I guess we both have something to celebrate. I got the job," I squealed.

"Whhaaatt. I told you that you would."

"Wait, you didn't have anything to do with this did you, Spence?"

I squinted at him while waiting for his answer.

"I promise you I had nothing to do with you getting that job, but you have to realize babe that you will be getting a lot of things because of who you are with, but I promise that you got the job by yourself. You know I was wanting you to come work with me."

"Ew, no. I be needing a break from you."

He placed his hand over his heart like he was really offended by what I said, knowing that he wasn't. He kissed me again before he left.

"Oh God! You two are disgusting," Lawrynn said and gagged.

"Stop hating. When one got the coins, we all got the coins," Russ said.

I rolled my eyes at them.

"Anyway, when are you going to tell the billionaire that you are to birth an heir," Law asked.

"Soon. Probably tonight. I'm scared because he hasn't talked about kids. I mean, we have, but he always would say, 'if I had kids' and not that he wanted kids."

They both rolled their eyes at me and claimed that I was being very dramatic, and I probably was, but still.

"Tell him, tonight. Look, I have to get back to work. Go home and kick off your shoes and think of a way to tell him," Russ said.

We all hugged and we parted ways. I thought of a creative way to tell him, but I couldn't think of anything. A week and a half ago, I started throwing up after I had some wings at 227. Law, Russ, and

I went straight to the nearest twenty-four hour CVS and got three pregnancy tests. I peed on all three of them in the store bathroom and found out that I was pregnant. I hadn't been to a doctor and confirmed it yet though. Maybe I could have gotten three false-positive tests.

€€€€

I was home and waiting on Spence to come in from work. I looked at the time and saw that he would be home in the next five minutes. I was nervous as hell because this man is probably going to make me get an abortion and kick me out and never talk to me again.

"Baby, I'm home." He walked in the kitchen and walked over to me to kiss me.

"What's wrong? I don't really feel the love right now."

"I'm nervous..."

"About what, baby? You're smart and you will do just fine on the new job."

"Not about that. About what's in the oven."

"You cooked? I don't smell anything," he said and walked over to the oven and opened it.

"Ain't nothing in here but a..." he said and whipped his head around towards me and started laughing. "Why you got a bun in the oven?" he asked and took a bite of the bun.

I thought that he had got it, but he didn't. I just stared at him because I couldn't believe that he was acting stupid... or maybe he wasn't acting.

"Repeat the question again, but slowly."

"Whyyy youuu gotttt aaaa buuunnnn inn theee ovennn?"

He did what I said and he still didn't get it, and at this point I wanted to beat him across the head with the bun that he was biting on. I sighed because I was getting annoyed that he wasn't getting it. I started rubbing my temples and he started laughing.

"Baby girl, I know you're pregnant. I knew last week because I knocked your purse over and the pregnancy tests fell out."

"Well, why didn't you say anything?!"

"I was waiting on you to tell me."

Anddd—"

"I'm not mad. I'm actually excited. I told my family already and everything because of how excited I was."

I smiled a little, but I hated that he told his family, because they hate me. Well his brother and dad are cool, but his mom and sister are upset. They swear that I'm only using Spence for his money and stuff, but I let Trena know that I do work unlike her, and she got mad about that and we almost came to blows at their brunch dinner. So, it's safe to say that I have never been back. His dad and brother come over on Saturdays and that's when I see them. They are actually nice to me.

"Look, don't worry about them. Trena is happy to be an aunt and my mom is happy to be a grandma. When the baby gets here, you'll have to beat them with a broom to keep them away from Quad."

"Quad?"

"Travis the fourth."

"If I have a girl?"

124

"Quaddeisha."

"I hate you so much, Travis Spencer the Third," I said and doubled over in laughter.

He came over and picked me up, prompting me to wrap my legs around him. He took me up to the bedroom where he slowly laid me down.

"God, I can't get over how beautiful you are," he groaned and loosened his tie.

I could never get used to him loosening his tie because that really does turn me on. He pulled his jacket off and threw it on the bed. He unbuckled his pants and pulled them down. It's been two months and I still can't get enough of him sexually. Me and this man literally have some type of sexual contact every day. Every day. It's perfect. Forty my ass... this man pleases me better than Malcolm could have on a very good and sober day.

He ran his cool hands up my shirt to squeeze my breasts. He leaned over to give me a long and very passionate kiss. He knew what his kisses did to me, so he knew that I was wet. He climbed between my legs and pushed himself in me without warning, making me gasp.

"I'm so addicted to you, Kriss," he whispered against my lips.

As always, I can't answer him when he is inside of me. I closed my eyes and enjoyed the wave that I was floating on.

"Open your eyes."

I opened them and stared deeply into his eyes. I still had the same connection we had the first night we made love.

"I love you, Kriss," he said, and my mouth fell open. "It's not because you're pregnant with my baby. It's this connection I felt with you the first night. My sprung ass wanted to tell you then but... I ain't want you to run away, but you did anyway. I don't want to ever lose you, Kriss Brown."

The tears pooled in my eyes as he was bringing me to an orgasm. The way he told me that he loved me, I knew that he wasn't lying.

"Hang on, mama. Don't tap out on me yet. Let me get mine," he whispered.

He put my legs on his shoulders and started to pummel me like he had something to prove. He leaned over, pushing my knees into my chest, and was going deeper than he ever had before.

"Ahhh, Travis. Just like that!" I shouted and dug my nails in his back.

"Like what? Like this?" he groaned and started going faster.

"Travisss!"

"What's up baby girl? You coming for me again?"

I closed my eyes so tight that I'm surprised my eyelids didn't tear in half.

"Nah, open your eyes. I wanna see those tears sliding down your face. Let me know I'm doing my job of pleasing my damn woman," he panted.

"TRAVIS PLEASEEEE!!!!" I screamed as I squirted on him.

"Oh yeah, I like that."

He didn't stop. He pulled out and turned me over and plunged deep in me before I could even think twice about it. Travis latched on to my waist and started to punish me... her. Travis loved rough sex and I was still trying to get used to it, but dirty talk made it easier.

"Arch your back, Krimson. I thought Krimson was nasty for me. Kriss told me that Krimson could take that wood."

"She cannnnn," I whined and tried to throw it back on him to match his strokes, but it wasn't no use.

"Why you whining? Stop whining and throw it back, Krimson," he groaned and smacked my ass twice.

"I can't take it, Travis. Ahhh."

"Oh you can't? You trying to tap out on me? Nah, ain't no tapping out. Take this shit."

He pulled my cheeks apart and thrust in and out of me so fast and I was squirting like a faucet. He was so deep in me that he was crossing my eyes. I was starting to see stars while he worked his magic behind me.

"Ohhh, thought you couldn't take it. Why you squirting on me, then?"

He pushed me forward, making me fall into the comforter. My body was flat but he pulled my ass up in the air, but he slowed his strokes down to a minimum pace. This was one of my favorite positions because he was hitting my g-spot at a different angle, making the orgasm that much more intense.

"Spence!" I cried out.

My body started to convulse as if I was having a seizure.

"That's right, baby. Give it to me because I'm definitely about to give it to you," he groaned.

His groans turned into light grunts as he erupted inside of me. He didn't pull out of me until he dropped everything inside of me. He fell next to me trying to catch his breath.

"Travis, I love you, too," I admitted.

The smile that widened across his face made my heart turn backflips in my chest.

We had showered and were back in bed cuddled up with each other. I was tracing his abs with my finger.

"Travis, do you think that we moved too fast? Two months in and we live together, and now I'm pregnant with your child."

"Nah, I don't. We moved at our own pace. We moved to our own pace and we are adults. I don't care about anything other people have to say our relationship. I'm happy and so are you, right?" he questioned and tilted his head to look down at me.

"Yes, I'm happy, Spence. I just—"

"Don't. Short story. My dad's parents met at age eighteen and got married six days later. They were together up until they turned ninety-five. My grandmother died on January fifth at 8:45 AM and my grandfather died on January fifth at 9:00 AM. It was like he knew that she had gone and he couldn't live without her. Love is love and doesn't have time restraints. My grandfather said that he knew she was the one for him after having one conversation with her. Just one conversation with her and he knew that he wanted to spend the rest of his life with her... and he did just that," he said. "There are people who date for years, get married, and divorced within two years, and there are people who get married after six days of knowing each other and stay married for seventy-seven years."

I couldn't help but cry at his grandparents' story. It sounded much like my mom and dad's story. He told me they got married after six months of knowing each other.

"Oh, baby, I didn't mean to make you cry. I was just telling you. Love has no time restraints. If you feel that shit, let that person know because life is short."

"You're right," I whispered.

We didn't say anything else for the rest of the night. I couldn't believe that I had fell for the exact man I said I never would date. A man with money because they are arrogant and mean, but Travis is neither of those things. Well he can be a little arrogant, but not much. For the first time in a very long time, I was happy.

EPILOGUE

Kriss

6 months later

These past six months have been great, and I was now sporting a belly that was carrying a precious little boy that Spence prayed for day in and day out. We went to the doctor a week after I revealed that I was pregnant and found out that I was six weeks pregnant, meaning that I had gotten pregnant the first or second night we had sex. I wondered if he knew what he was doing from the very beginning.

I rolled over and saw that Travis was no longer in bed. I figured that he had gotten up to go work-out. I got up, took a shower, and went downstairs.

"Surpriseee! Happy birthday, Kriss!"

I jumped at the loud cheers. I wasn't expecting anything spectacular because I told Spence not to go all out for my birthday. His family was there and my dad and friends were there at the table surrounding a cake. It took a few months, but Trena and his mom came around. We weren't buddy buddy but we weren't mean to each other anymore. They had finally come around and accepted that Spence and

I were together and were going to be together for a while... forever, I hope. His assistant Zahara was here and her sister Jaquel was here as well. He told me about their tryst and he didn't get rid of her because she had been handling her job well. I'll still be watching her, and the first time I think that she is trying to step out that stylist box, she'll be jobless in a matter of seconds. There were also a few of the women architects that I had made friends with at Ground-Up just from being there with Spence all the time.

Spence didn't want me working so much because of the pregnancy so I was working part time. He told me that I was going to have to put in a leave of absence once I get nine months pregnant because he didn't want me away from the house when I was that far along. I left 227 completely and Nardo was heated and tried to talk about that contract, but after Spence beat his ass and then gave him his little money, he ripped up the contract. I don't even stop by, but I still meet up with JuJu, Miguel, and Tya from time to time. Spence had already started looking into hiring nannies and security and everything. Now that was overwhelming. There wasn't anyone more excited than my dad to become a grandpa. I gave my dad a hug and he rained kisses down on my cheeks. I hugged and thanked everybody for coming because I was truly surprised.

"Blow the candles out, Kriss. Close your eyes and make a wish first," Spence said.

I closed my eyes and made a wish. I wish that everyone stays happy like we are and that Spence and I have a healthy baby along with a healthy love life. I wish that my friends found love and happiness, and the same for my dad. After my multiple wishes, I opened my eyes and blew out the candles while everyone cheered. I held my stomach because Quad had kicked me.

When I turned around, Travis was on one knee. My hand went to my heart because that was the real surprise.

"Travis..." I called his name just above a whisper.

Grabbing my hand, he started to rub my fingers.

"Kriss Brown, you are one amazing woman. I never saw myself getting married or even having kids, but then you came along and changed all of that for me. I knew from the first day when you told me that you wanted to carve my heart out and blend it up with your shake, I wanted you, but after the first time we connected, I knew I needed you. If it wasn't for you, I wouldn't have ever taken the proper steps to become a chef. If it wasn't for you, I wouldn't have been able to fulfill my lifelong dream. Kriss, I need you in my life forever. Please, do me the honor of being Mrs. Travis Spencer the Third," he said and opened the box.

The sun hit that rock and it nearly blinded me. My mouth opened, but nothing came out. I was shocked. I looked at my dad and he nodded his head 'yes' and my friends did the same thing. I looked back at him with tears in my eyes.

"I'm scared," I whispered.

"Me too."

"What about—"

"Don't."

"I can't afford—"

"Who said you have to afford anything? I got us... forever. My money is your money. I got enough for all three of us," he said and placed his hand on my protruding stomach.

"Yes, Travis. I'll spend the rest of my life with you," I finally said.

He slid the heavy ass rock on my hand and I instantly fell in love with him all over again. He stood and gave me a long, sloppy kiss. Trevor started playing music and everyone started mingling with each other while I continued to stare at my ring.

"Girl! We made it!" Russ cheered as he approached me.

"Shut-up Russ. Girl, this ring is so HOT! I'm sure that ring is larger than Kim Kardashian's ring. Anyways, I'm about to go see what Trevor hitting for."

"Never change, Law," I said, and her and Russ walked away from me.

Spence came up behind me and wrapped his arm around my neck.

"I'm so in love with you, baby girl."

"I guess falling in love with a billionaire wasn't so bad," I replied.

THE END

MESSAGE FROM BIANCA

Hey Y'all! Thank you all so much for the love and constant support. This is the first time I ever tried strictly romance, so please let me know how I did with a review, an inbox message, or a comment in my readers group. I was so scared to release this because this is way out of my expertise so I decided to explore with a short story. Thank you for staying with me along my growing writing journey. As always, I have to thank God for blessing me with the talent to be able to make you experience every emotion. My Royalty sisters, I love you all so much for being such a constant support, and being such a strong group of women.

BriAnn & Deshon & Tya: In an industry full of shady individuals, I know that I can always count on you three. Thank you for always motivating me and pushing me to be the best that I can be. You are the best group of gals that I could ever ask for. Love you all sooo much!

Last, but certainly not least, I MUST thank my readers. You guys give me the strength I need to continue to write. Reading your reviews, and inbox messages, makes me feel so loved. Thank you for taking a chance on me! Hope I continue to make you fall in love with my writing.

With Love,

Bianca Xaviera

CONNECT WITH ME ON SOCIAL MEDIA

Join *Bee's Literary Beehive* Readers Group:

https://www.facebook.com/groups/AuthoressBianca/

Facebook Like Page: www.facebook.com/AuthoressBianca

Instagram: @BiancaXaviera_

Other *Novels by Bianca*

https://www.amazon.com/author/bianca

Subscribe to my Website for Sneak Peeks and Short Stories:

www.authoressbianca.com

Text ROYALTY to 42828 to join our mailing list!

To submit a manuscript for our review, email us at
submissions@royaltypublishinghouse.com

Text RPHCHRISTIAN to 22828 for our
CHRISTIAN ROMANCE novels!

Text RPHROMANCE to 22828 for our
INTERRACIAL ROMANCE novels!